OUTSIDE THE LAW

Out behind the bunkhouses, the glow of his cigarette showed the concern on Nick Dunn's face as he took in the new arrivals. He resisted the urge to get in closer, to pick up on their conversation, muttering to himself, "Easy."

But the tension still remained in him, and it was something he couldn't shake. There was one amongst this bunch of westerners, a big man who'd kept eyeballing him in the bunkhouse . . . he looked like a gunman. And Nick Dunn's face adorned wanteds papering every sheriff's office from up here down to the nations.

His very life depended on hiding the fact that Nick Dunn was the notorious Starky True.

Every western lawman had gotten the word—shoot on sight!

ROBERT KAMMEN

OUTSIDE THE LAW

ZEBRA BOOKS
KENSINGTON PUBLISHING CORP.

ZEBRA BOOKS are published by

Kensington Publishing Corp.
850 Third Avenue
New York, NY 10022

First Printing: September, 1995

Printed in the United States of America

PROLOGUE

For several years stock detectives, deputy sheriffs and detectives had been trying to locate gunman Starky True. But he seemed to have vanished, with lawmen concluding that True had fled to the Southwest and had allied himself with one of the several bands of desperadoes operating in southern Utah and Nevada.

The charge hanging over Starky True was that of dry-gulching George Wellman, foreman of the "Hoe" outfit, on the Powder River. Shortly after this, True, well known as a gunman and killer as well as a rustler, had disappeared. Now, up in Buffalo at a gathering of lawmen, the outlaw's name had come under discussion.

"He could be dead."

"Not that weaselly scumbag."

"About the kindest epithet I can hang on Starky True," said Deputy Sheriff Pete Briscoe, "is of his being a pothole on the road to nowhere."

Grim laughter rippled around the lobby of the Owen Wister Hotel. They'd come from all over Wyoming and southern Montana, men earmarked by the rigors of their lawkeeping trade. You could see it in their eyes that all this talk about Starky True was stinging at their pride. The back-shooting outlaw should have been pushing up daisies a long time ago, and they knew it. The morning meeting had just broken up, with some of them hanging on in the lobby for a quick smoke while others were chowing down in the dining room. One of their reasons for coming here was to give support to Johnson County ranchers fighting not only rustlers but sodbusters laying claim to some choice bottom land. Of course, it didn't hurt any that the Stockmen's Association was picking up the tab for their hotel rooms and incidental expenses.

"Yup," said stock inspector Al Novotny, "a thousand dollars to the man bringin' in Starky." Taking a last puff on his hand-rolled, he was about to flick it out the open lobby door when his gaze landed on a horseman swinging out of the saddle. A grin broke out as he exclaimed, "I'll be damned, I didn't think W.D. Smith was gonna show."

A few came up to gaze out at W.D. "Billy" Smith using his hat to brush trail dust from his clothes as he came under the shadow of the overhanging porch and entered the lobby. Now others moved in closer to welcome Smith, chief stock inspector for the Montana association. He was a bulky, dark-haired man and a former U.S. marshal. He worked out of Billings, and before that, Miles City. He said dryly, "I figured you bunch of freeloaders would show up."

"The hell you say, Billy," said a deputy sheriff. "How you been, as it's been a spell?"

"At least I'm feelin' a mite better than Starky True."

A sudden tension filled the lobby, and then someone said, "We was just talkin' about Starky."

"Damndest story," muttered W.D. Smith. "Some of it's my fault, I reckon, for not checkin' things out . . ."

"Spit it out, Billy, what about Starky True—"

"Here everyone figured him to be down in Old Mexico or points further south. While all the while—well, I reckon those wantin' to hear about Starky'll have to hear it in the barroom. As this old hoss has a powerful thirst." He broke away to the right and down a short hallway, with everyone who'd been in the lobby scrambling behind.

After he'd hammered down two quick shot glasses of prime whiskey at the bar, stock inspector Billy Smith turned and said gravely to his fellow lawmen, "I don't reckon Starky True played me for a sucker. Down here you know him as a gunhand and . . ."

"And purequill scum. But go on, Billy."

W.D. "Billy" Smith ambled over to the closest table and sought a chair, the tide of lawmen coming to circle around, and he said, "Where to begin? I expect that'll have to be away up at the N Bar N outfit. Couple of years ago it was, late spring when this cowpoke rode in askin' to be put on the payroll . . ."

ONE

Even the horses bunched up in the corrals had caught the scent of anticipation shared by the N Bar N cowpokes about heading out from the home buildings to start the spring roundup. They'd just come off a hard winter, and every rancher from the Bearpaws looming just east clear over to the Rockies was deeply worried about what winter kill had done to their herds. Because of this an open-range roundup would take place, wherein several ranches would join forces to conduct spring branding.

Just last week while attending a stockman's association meeting held over at Box Elder, foreman Tom Wilson had been nominated to the job of roundup boss. It wasn't exactly a job he relished taking on, though he'd buried his reluctance behind a nod of acceptance. Everyone out here knew that Tom Wilson made most of the major decisions for the N Bar N since the manager of the ranch, a Havre lawyer, rarely ventured out. The ranch was owned by a Chicago consortium, some of whom had come out a couple of years ago to play at being cattlemen. Except for the Jinglebob spread farther west near Shelby, Tom Wilson ramrodded the biggest cattle spread in northern Montana. He got paid accordingly, otherwise he would have left long ago, and he still might, as he still held to the notion of being a rancher himself.

He knew no other life than ranching. At thirty-five, he was a solid, square-jawed man with steady brown eyes. When he was cowboying he could raise cane with the best of them, and occasionally Tom Wilson would get to feeling his oats over at Box Elder or Big Sandy. But not to the extent of calling down shame on himself or the N Bar N. Over in Box Elder, too, lived Vivian McCauley, widowed going on three years now and about as handsome a woman as he'd ever seen. She had a few beaus, but she didn't seem to be in any particular hurry to hitch up with one of them. Could be none of them quite measured up, and Tom wondered if he did.

Every day more riders kept coming in, some who'd been let go last fall and men he'd never laid eyes on before seeking a riding job. Behind Tom Wilson lay the rambling, two-story gabled house. It needed a coat of paint and some siding boards replaced, and caulking added around the window frames. During the winter it seemed every time a hard wind came out of the northwest, which to Tom Wilson had seemed like every damned day, a cold chill crept into the house even though the fireplace and kitchen stove had been throwing out heat. He was of a mind to just put up a low, fieldstone house with its front door quartering off to the southeast yonder where a low bluff thrust up as a wind barrier. Not only was this big, clapboard relic of a house wind-leaky, but it stood all by its lonesome on a knoll. To provide a view for the wife of the rancher who'd owned it before.

He began ambling down toward the corrals. There were five of them, all being used to hold horses. Weathered sheds and a large barn made up the home buildings, along with a smithy, the tack house and a pair of bunkhouses. He shared the main house with the cook and two helpers taken on now that the N Bar N was crewing up. The anxiety of just getting out there was pushing at him, too, and he eyed the reach of prairie beyond the barren ground flowing around the buildings. Cannily he knew that time was measured in a cow camp not by calendar dates, but by the "comin' grass," when the range began to green up. It showed signs of it, in patches, and Tom Wilson was hoping, as was every other cattleman, for a real soaker.

"It'll come a'fore long," he muttered as watched one of his hands taking out the high jinks of one of the broncs in his string.

The waddy, Clemet Hall, was glued to the saddle of his semi-bronc, a big gelding, as it bucked around the circling interior of the large corral. This was a cowhand's way of giving a bronc like this a few lessons in higher education of just what it meant to be saddle-broke. These were the last few days before they headed out, waiting for the clan to gather, as it was known. There'd be a lot of romp and frolic because these cowhands knew there'd be no play after the work started. Yet each man knew the work he was to do and made all the preparations for it. He overhauled his personal outfit and put in repair; his rope was limbered up and his straps softened and his wearing gear put in readiness. Just as important were his weapons, generally a Colt .45 with matching slugs for his rifle—as there was still some Indian trouble, from the Blackfeet and lesser tribes. Sometimes Tom Wilson would haze some cattle to the nearby Rocky Boy Reservation as a peace offering. But his greatest worry was the rustlers, the renegade whites, who caused the most trouble.

"That smithy of yours, Tom, shore did a fine job of platin' my hosses," said Wyman Pruitt as he returned the foreman's smile. Pruitt was a lanky, graying man whose left arm hung out at an angle from his side due to the fact it had been broken and never set properly. He had been idling around Box Elder, semi-retired as he called it, when Tom Wilson had picked Pruitt to be tallyman. One reason was that Wyman Pruitt was honest, and, too, he knew how to use the working end of a lead pencil. "Couple of riders comin' in, Tom."

Hitching his hat back, the foreman followed the slant of Pruitt's gaze to the northeast. Coming from that way meant someone from either Box Elder or Havre. They weren't riding together, as one of them was back at least a couple of miles. He had sixteen on the payroll, was hoping to add at least five more. Be another half hour, Tom mused, before the first rider would be in, and he swung his attention to the next corral and upon tall, stony-faced Henry Thompson, known in these parts as "Long Henry." Thompson had ridden in a week ago looking for work, and Tom had taken the man on even though he knew that Long Henry Thompson wore a gun marked by four notches. Yet knowing Thompson to be a superior roper, Tom had told the man that as long as he kept his temper and guns under control he could work for the N Bar N.

"Maybe I made a mistake, Wyman . . ."

"Yeah?"

"About Henry Thompson . . ."

"Time'll tell, I reckon. Could be, too, Tom, that a lawman'll ride in one day and take that worry off your hands."

The first rider proved to be longtime N Bar N waddy Les Aston coming back—as he shouted in response to a where-the-hell-you-been—from having wintered down in Santa Fe. He was a musician of sorts, kicking out showy tunes on a guitar or banjo, and with a bull-froggy baritone voice that set a man's teeth to a'grittin' when he sang. A deep tan made Aston's teeth flash whiter as he spotted the N Bar N foreman. "Would'a been here sooner, Tom, but . . ."

A waddy catcalled out, "But there was this sweet little thing I encountered along the way."

Les Aston swung down and grasped the foreman's rocklike hand and said anxiously, "You do need another hand? At least one that appreciates the finer things in life."

"You know I do. A week, I make it, an' we'll be pullin' out. Maybe tonight you can honor us lowly and uneducated cowpokes with a song or two, Mr. Aston. That's right, you get paid for doin' this now. Wyman, seems we'll have to pass a tin cup around to help defray expenses for this musical shindig."

"Nope, from now on it comes with the job, Mr. Wilson," Aston replied.

"That's mighty noble of you, Mr. Aston. An' glad you're back." Tom Wilson moved away as Aston walked his horse over to shake hands with others. The second horseman had now reached the outer buildings. He was a stranger to Tom, but nevertheless rode with the grace of a Westerner, the clothes the stranger wore of an expensive cut. This time the foreman went out alone to meet the incoming rider, the late afternoon sun at his back and elongating his shadow toward the east.

"Afternoon," the rider said cordially. "From your description you're Mr. Wilson." Reining up, he swung down slowly to come around the horse, holding out a wrinkled envelope. "This is from Mr. Glendenning."

He recognized the lawyer's handwriting on the envelope, and when he opened the letter, he scanned its contents. "So he wants me to give you a job. Nick Dunn, uh?"

"Yessir, all of us Dunns grew up down in southern Utah. The way that desert is down there, Mr. Wilson, raisin' cattle is a chore a lot fail at."

"Tough times have hit us, too, Nick."

Hastily the newcomer said, "It don't matter none what job you hand me durin' spring roundup. As I've done them all . . . all 'cept cookin'."

"No, wouldn't want you to do that. Truth is, I need a few more good hands. From the looks of you, and your hoss, you can handle that." Turning, he waved Wyman Pruitt over. "Wyman'll get you rigged up in the bunkhouse. T'morrow mornin' they'll be bringing in the rough string remuda. Those hosses have had a whole winter to figure out new ways to ease a man out of the saddle. But they're solid stock, and I reckon you can manage to pick your own string, Nick, same's the others."

Just shy of sundown Tom Wilson was pleased to see pushing up dust from the west some old friends in the form of two ranchers riding amongst the cowpokes they'd brought along. He pulled the brim of his hat down more to shade his squinting eyes from the low-lying sun where he sat on the front porch of the main house. With him was Wyman Pruitt, who commented dryly, "I expect more'll be comin' in the next few days."

"Yeah," Tom agreed, "to add their two cents to just how to

hold the spring roundup." He'd risen from a caneback chair, as had Pruitt, and they moved to stand by the porch steps as the cavalcade of seven Westerners rode up, with Wilber Farley blowing cigarette smoke out through his shaggy handlebar mustache. Farley had brought along three of his men, who were holding back a little and gazing toward the bunkhouse where some N Bar N hands had gathered. The other rancher, Kelly Riggins, sat there grinning as he let his fellow rancher have the first go with words.

And Wilber Farley said, "Couldn't hold out there any longer, Tom. So I rode over and talked Riggins inta taggin' along. The place looks good." He was a large man, wide-spanned through the shoulders and wearin' old work clothes, a beat-up Stetson and worn leather coat, and scuffed boots coming up over faded Levi's. It didn't make no matter to Farley what he wore, even if it was to go to some highfalutin meeting over at Havre or church. His only concession to his missus's complaints that he look halfway presentable was to scrape away the chin whiskers. He owned a fair-sized spread, the W Slash F, which was laid out northerly along the Canadian border.

Kelly Riggins, a dignified-looking man with a wiry frame, ranched more to the southwest and in the shadow of the Rockies. About ten years ago a green-broke horse had pitched Riggins out of the saddle, and he'd come out of it with a broken jaw. Ever since, he spoke slower, spacing out his words so that each one sounded like a sentence. He said to his men, "You boys go over and check in at the bunkhouse. So, Tom, and you, Wyman, good to set eyes on you boys again." As Riggins swung down, he passed his reins to one of Wilber Farley's hands, who trailed the horse over to the corral. Another waddy tended to Farley's large mottled gray bronc. The ranchers eased onto the porch as the front door opened and one of the cook's helpers came out to place the tray he carried on a round table set in one corner of the porch.

"Whiskey," grinned Wilber Farley—"I could sure use some

of that Forty-rod. As the missus raises heck if I pack any along home. So what's the word, Tom, how many pooled in this year?"

"You'n Kelly here make nine—I reckon there'll be more."

Out beyond the bunkhouses the glow of his cigarette showed the concern on Nick Dunn's face as he took in the new arrivals. He resisted the urge to get in closer to pick up on their conversation, muttering to himself, "Easy." But the tension still remained in him, and it was something he couldn't shake. Northern Montana wasn't all that far from a place where he was wanted by the law. So far everyone here was a complete stranger, but chances were someone had seen his face adorning the wanteds papering every sheriff's office from up here down to the Nations.

There was one amongst this bunch of Westerners, a big man, who'd kept eyeballing him in the bunkhouse shortly before he'd come out here to make himself comfortable on this rusty seat centered on an old metal hay rack, a device that was pulled by a team of horses during haying season. He just wanted to be alone, to collect his thoughts, and to decide if this was a good place to hole up. One of the hands had informed him the big man's name was Henry Thompson.

"Got him tallied as a gunman."

And maybe this big galoot had Nick Dunn marked the same way. Since that was what he was, and more. Being a rustler and killer among other things. The rich, aromatic flavor of the tobacco he had in his tailor-made brought a pleased glint to Dunn's eyes as he took in the lay of this place. Right away he'd detected in N Bar N foreman Tom Wilson touches of a steely character and the fact Wilson liked things tidied up, be it these buildings or just how a man took care of his own possible bag and horse. The segundo would soon learn that he hadn't made a mistake in hiring Nick Dunn, as cowboying was a big part of his life, too. The trick, and a hard-learned one at that, was to fit in with the other cowpokes, melt into obscurity, which sometimes meant tackling the tougher chores. And he would, for his very life depended on no one finding out that he was really the notorious Starky True.

Every western lawman had gotten the word—shoot on sight!

Back some from the main house and downslope, just this side of some willowy brush, flames eddied away from a barbecue pit. The cook was out there jabbering with some waddies while his helpers were passing back and forth bringing out more food to place on a couple of tables that had been set up. More cowpokes were drifting over, and Dunn had it in mind to mosey over, but this inner caution kept him seated on the rake. Like everyone else, he'd shucked his gunbelt.

Nick Dunn began going over the circuitous route that had brought him here, first west almost into Idaho, and back around the provinces of southern Canada and to Havre, where he'd become acquainted with a lawyer named Ralph Glendenning.

It turned out they had much in common, gambling and loose women, and then one day the lawyer had let it out he was also business manager for the N Bar N ranch. The job Nick was offered contained a provision that he keep an eye on ranch foreman Tom Wilson. He remembered the hostility that had flared in Glendenning's eyes. Gazing again at the flames radiating away from the barbecue pit, Nick Dunn was wondering if he'd made a mistake by coming out here. Even though he was on the dodge and down to his last few dollars.

"Time will tell," he muttered, as tallyman Wyman Pruitt began ambling over from the bunkhouse.

"Well, Mr. Dunn, you'll find you didn't make a mistake by coming out here. The N Bar's one of the finest spreads in these parts . . . an' Tom Wilson's easy to work for."

"What I've been hearing." Dunn eased off the seat and dropped his cigarette butt to grind it out with a boot heel. They fell into step, angling by the bunkhouse as they chatted. "Tell me, Mr. Pruitt, does this lawyer, Glendenning, ever come out here?"

"You'd have to ask Tom about that. Strange setup, as by rights it should be Tom Wilson in charge of the N Bar. As he does all the work anyway. Why'd you ask about this Havre lawyer?"

"Just that he was kind enough to give me a job. That roastin' side of beef's got a right tangy smell to it . . ."

"One thing about the N Bar is you ain't saddled with a bunch of plugs in yer string." The cowhand's eyes slid away from Nick Dunn to the remuda of around a hundred horses being hazed toward the home buildings. The sun hadn't risen yet, and it was cold. The cowpokes were standing away from the corrals which had their pole gates open.

One thing Nick Dunn cautioned himself about as he put on his other glove was to just let the natural order of things happen. Like everyone else, he wasn't wearing a gunbelt. This morning they'd be picking out horses for their strings. The older hands would have first choice, a string consisting of morning horses and afternoon horses, amongst which would be a good rope horse, a cutting horse, a night horse, and in trail days each man liked to have a good river horse. Also, every man was allowed all the broncs he wanted to ride. Therefore, as Nick Dunn was aware, each man generally had several half-broke horses in his mount. They were mostly used on short rides and gradually broken, for in actual cow work a bronc was worthless. If the boss thought a horse had the makings of a good cow horse, he tried to assign it to a rider he knew would train it right. He knew a man had to have more sense than the horse if he was able to teach the animal cow sense.

Along with the others, Nick began hazing the horses into the pair of larger corrals, the dust kicking up and horses wheeling about in the confusion of which corral to go into. The horses were thinned out from just coming in off winter range, but were as good a bunch of mounts as he'd ever seen. He eyed one or two he'd like to rope into his string, the bulk of the horses solid colors as preferred by most cowpokes. In Nick was a sense of expectancy, for not only would be have to rope out his horses, but saddle them and let them buck out their winter wildness. He said to the hand Leroy Green, out of Big Timber, "Like the hosses, I've got a lot of kinks to work out."

"You ain't no orphan in that d'partment, Nick. There's some wild broncs in amongst them; bein' new out here, you'll pro'bly be stuck with some."

"Way it is," Nick said laconically. And as the day wore on, he found that the focus of everyone was centered on roping out horses. He began to relax while tending to the chore of helping out at the smaller roping corrals where snub posts had been driven into the ground in the middle of each corral. A horse brought there to be ridden would oftentimes react wildly to the touch of a saddle blanket, and Nick and others would help get the animal saddled, then hurry to straddle corral posts as the horse was turned loose to buck away.

After the noon break it was his turn to pick a string out of what was left, that being twenty-one geldings for the three of them. They took turns roping out horses and, when they did, set the horses apart in other corrals. He began exchanging small talk with Sid Osborne, a newcomer as he was, and with affable Les Aston. "Take a man like me, Les, just an ordinary cowpuncher needin' a job like this as he's got no other skills. But you, with your guitar an' all, you could make a pretty penny just plunkin' away at that . . ."

"Well, Nick, bright lights and pretty señoritas pale after a while. Sure, there's some money in it. Perils in it, too, like a man becomin' a mean ol' drunk after a time." He opened the gate of a breaking corral and came in behind Nick, bringing a haltered horse, a bay, up to the snubbing post. Behind them came Sid Osborne hefting Nick's saddle and blanket.

"One thing," Aston went on, "I reckon you know Thompson's been throwin' you some bad-awful looks. You run into Long Henry before?"

"Nope," he said truthfully, "Thompson's a complete stranger; maybe he don't like the way I wear my hat. He'll get over it." He took the blanket from Osborne and eased it over the wide back of the bronc, which punched in against the snubbing post snorting its uncertainties. Then he swung the saddle up, and the bronc reared up and snapped out at him with a foreleg which he managed to dodge.

"What'sa matter, Dunn, you can't handle a gentle hoss like that?"

The words were flung at him by Long Henry Thompson, who, Nick found when he glanced that way, had eased up with most of the others to watch the action. Nick shot a glance at Les Aston holding onto the bronc's bridle, and grinned as if to say to hell with Thompson's jabbing words. Thompson and the others would find that Nick Dunn could control his temper and was slow to frame words. For Nick knew that his staying free depended on him melting peaceably into the woodwork of the N Bar N. He managed to cinch the saddle of the bronc stamping its hooves and still fighting the bit in its foaming mouth. Bracing to swing into the saddle, he took in the corded muscles rippling under the dark brown skin telling him of the immense power building up to explode.

Quickly he swung aboard the bay, and just as quickly Aston pulled the blinder away and let go of the bridle. The next instant the bronc was catting around in a tight circle and humping into a high series of bucks that took it and its rider slamming into one side of the small corral. Nick ignored the pain radiating from his right leg, and the saddle horn, for to grab for it would tell the onlookers and especially Long Henry Thompson that he'd thrown in the towel. He forgot everything when the bronc came down on all four hooves, slamming into the hard-packed ground so forcefully Nick was almost damned certain the horse had dug a hole. Then it was skying again and bucking around the corral to the pleasure of everyone watching, even ranch foreman Tom Wilson, who'd just come up.

He didn't remember much else of the ride, just that suddenly the bronc had quit bucking and had responded to his tug on the reins as he shouted out for someone to open the gate. He brought the bronc galloping out past the other corrals and down an easterly running lane to about a quarter of a mile, before spurring it around but coming back at an easy canter. The horse was a four-year-old and, Nick reckoned, just starting to catch on to the rudiments of being a good cow horse. And its name he'd been told was Sparky.

This was the last horse he'd have to ride today as it filled out his string of seven, and he was glad this day was about over. Tomorrow and the next few days all of them would take their horses out to work them, and maybe round up some cattle holding in closer to the buildings. Coming in on the corrals, he heard Tom Wilson say amiably, "Reckon you'll do at that, Mr. Dunn. This hoss, Sparky, he's a bit raw like the other broncs we've got."

"Come fall he'll be some cow hoss, Mr. Wilson." Nick, smiling as Wilson turned and moved away, looked over at Thompson, who was still holding by the roping corral and chatting with another cowpoke. *There'll be trouble,* Nick Dunn mused wearily, *as this Long Henry ain't the kind to let go of things.* The man was at least five inches taller than Nick, and solid, but from what he'd been told, Thompson liked to use his guns.

Nick brought the bay over to the water trough, where he swung down and let the horse drink. Looking about, he noticed that most of the hands were ambling toward the bunkhouses, the business of picking out their strings over, and supper in the offing. He returned the horse to the corrals and removed the saddle, ignoring the boring eyes of Long Henry Thompson as the man ambled toward the bunkhouses. He began using the blanket to give the horse a rubdown, speaking softly to the bronc as he did, and it stood docilely.

"Yup, Sparky," Nick Dunn said bitterly, softly, "this Long Henry, man knows I'm a gunfighter same's him. Will he let it rest there? Maybe others out here are ridin' the owlhoot trail, too. Dunno, Sparky, but all the same, it's best we tread warily around Thompson, or at least try to. . . ."

TWO

By next Thursday, less than a week after Nick Dunn had hired on, the N Bar N was pulling out to the northwest. The N Bar had furnished a chuck wagon and bedroll wagon, along with an extra wagon that would be used to hold the calves that were unable to keep up when the ranch hands began gathering cattle. During the day, as they moseyed their horses toward the rendezvous point—the junction of Coulee Creek and the Marias River—they hooked up with small groups of riders.

Every time they met a new bunch, Nick Dunn kept his eyes riveted to the newcomers, in the fear someone would recognize him. But so far it had proved out that most of the cowhands were old northern Montana hands, and he began to shed a few worries. Out here he wore a gunbelt, but wore no coat in the rising heat of this windy spring day. Alongside rode Osborne and Aston and beyond them a couple more cowpokes. They were still cutting across N Bar land, where young grass rippled greenly under sunlight. Away to the north and at least three miles in front of them flowed the remuda. The wagons had pulled out before sunup and at the rendezvous point would be joined by two more chuck wagons. As Tom Wilson had told them, this had proved out to be the granddaddy of all spring roundups—a makeup of eleven ranches.

Pushing along silently, and gripping the remnants of a tailor-made, Nick got to musing about another spring gathering such as this. Only then he'd been with a bunch of "sooners," men who worked the range before the official roundup date. That time it had been some smaller ranchers running a shotgun wagon. They'd been able to apply running irons to many strays and mavericks to which they weren't legally entitled. What it had been had been out-and-out rustling, and he'd barely humped out of there ahead of the law. Ever since, he'd left rustling to others, to hire out his gun to the highest bidder. Forget that, and Wyoming, Nick cautioned himself.

At around eleven Tom Wilson called a powwow with the other ranchers. They were coming across a few cattle, and the idea was to have the cowpokes fan out and drive the cattle ahead of them, so that the mavericks and calves sprinkled in with the cows could be tended to in the morning. The meeting breaking up, Wilson spurred his horse over to tell his N Bar hands the way of it for the rest of the day.

Then he drew Nick aside and said, "My wrangler, Arte Reese, is ailin', Nick. I checked on him a little while ago and it don't look good. But Arte said he'd stick it out long's he could. That wranglin' job of tendin' to the remuda don't stand high in a cow camp. An' I was gonna have Wyman Pruitt take over, but Wyman's pretty much set as tallyman . . ."

"Sure, come mornin' if Arte isn't any better, I'll take over as wrangler," said Nick in a pleasant manner.

"You sure, Nick? Some 'pokes'll rather shag out than take on that chore."

Nodding around the smile of acceptance, he knew there was no other choice open to him. And one good thing might come out of it; it would keep him away from Henry Thompson, as they'd be sure to run into one another while rounding up cattle. The problem was the chores of the wrangler included helping the cook pack the camp plunder when it came time to move the chuck wagon, and this roustabout job, as Nick knew, wasn't held to be very elevating. That was why the wrangler wasn't considered to amount to much.

He also knew that when more ranchers and cowpokes joined the roundup, it would swell the size of the remuda. It was the chore of the wagon boss to count the remuda every day to check on the wrangler, and if a horse chanced to be missing, Nick would catch sorry hell from everyone. About the only blessing to the job was that he wouldn't have to stand killpecker guard all night. After the cook called him in the morning, a smart wrangler could take his own time crawling out stretching and scratching to enjoy that first cigarette and cup of coffee. Filled with these thoughts, he spurred after the N Bar hands pushing westerly into a wide draw.

Sprinkled in with the N Bar cattle they began hazing were other brands, all unfamiliar to Nick Dunn. Clouds thinly streaked the late afternoon sky, and sunlight came lancing down in golden streaks which fell warmly upon their shoulders. Just being on the move, even if it meant the rigors of spring branding, brought pleased glints to the men's eyes. Way to the west Nick could make out Long Henry Thompson spurring with some other cowpokes toward another long draw choked with brush.

He said to Les Aston, "I guess Thompson'll really lay it to me now, Les."

"How's that?"

"Wilson asked me to take over the remuda for Arte Reese; guess Reese is ailin' some."

"That old fart should never have come along—but I reckon old Arte wanted one last hurrah as a sort of workin' hand. Don't feel bad, Nick, as Long Henry picks on everyone. Someday he'll get his damn-fool head blown off doin' it, though. You said you hailed from Nevada, Nick?"

"So long ago I can't remember much about it. But, yup, barren a place as you can find." He pointed toward some brush beginning to stir in a draw they were honing in on, and from here he let Aston and Osborne pull out ahead in pursuit of some cattle, glad the conversation had broken away, even though he could tell that neither man entertained any suspicions about him being a gunhand.

About an hour later they were coming in on the herd ground where cattle were bunched up and grazing as dusk started to settle. From here they simply let the cattle they'd found drift in slowly with the main herd, a small one of approximately a thousand head. Camp fires were going around the three chuck wagons and the one big rope corral containing about thirty horses. Tomorrow the real work would start, and from what Tom Wilson had told them, it was a task that could consume two or three weeks.

Instead of riding in with the others, Nick reined off a little as he checked out the faces of those already in camp. All it would take was for one man to make out who he really was, and he'd be forced to find another place to hide out. Long ago he'd given up the useless task of cursing out those Wyoming lawmen for clinging so tenaciously to his past. They didn't have any hard evidence against him in the killing of Hoe outfit foreman George Wellman. Maybe if he'd stayed put . . . well, with his reputation Nick knew he would have been dead and buried a long time ago. The fact was he had killed Wellman, had spent the dinero. It was his plan someday to look up Brady Summit, the rancher who'd hired him to kill Wellman. He could sure as sin blackmail the man, or even spill what he knew to a U.S. marshal in exchange for clemency. Which he doubted strongly was what would happen.

"Nope, mercy ain't a word those law gents know."

The Rockies to the west cut away the glare of the sun even though day was reluctant to give way to night. Twilight held in as cowpokes found places to stash their bedrolls, under shrub trees and cottonwoods. Afterward they renewed old friendships while waiting for the cook to ring out it was time to chow down.

Nick Dunn let the talk of Les Aston, and Osborne, and a few other hands swirl around him as he used a bit of cloth to clean the dust of day from his Winchester. He tended to the care of his guns more-so at times than the horse he was forking, since his life depended on a weapon not jamming when it was sorely needed. He sat straddling his saddle, with his bedroll rolled out a few feet away from brush lining the creek. From here, if the cattle took the notion to stampede, it was a short distance to the rope corral holding their horses. A few hands were still out watching the herd grazing peacefully in the gathering darkness, the glow of the camp fires reminding Nick Dunn of the brief interval of time he'd spent in the army. He hadn't liked bivouacking or taking orders and one day had simply cut out. He doubted if the army was even interested in him now, and didn't care. Nor about his immediate family or any other kin. The important thing was survival, which to him meant keeping out of the clutches of the law, and living the high life when he could.

By nature he was quiet, liked to hold back and let others take that first risk, and if it panned out, he would then jump on the bandwagon. The money he'd made from his sundry crimes had gone mostly to the girls in the cribs, and a helluva lot more he'd lost at the gaming tables. Right now he could sure use some rotgut to cut away the slight tang of dust in his mouth, but taking along whiskey on a roundup was the same as a 'poke ridin' a mare—two things that spelled trouble.

"You're awful quiet, Nick . . ."

"Just gettin' my bearings," he said amiably. "One thing, I've heard of some holdin' big roundups before, but . . ."

"But this one is big awright, Nick, coverin' one hunk of territory. Clear up to Canada one way; then cuttin' west just shy of Shelby." Les Aston's words fell away when three riders loomed up and came past one of the bedroll wagons, one of them being Henry Thompson. Aston looked at Nick Dunn, who was watching Thompson carefully, and knew before this roundup was over these two would tangle. Aston's worries then turned to the bottle Thompson had sneaked along, and had been nursing during the day as he rode. He thought, *man's got a mean streak as is.* And then wondered if he should pass on what he knew to Tom Wilson. Or let it pass as Wilson would probably give Thompson his walking papers.

Resting the hand that held the cloth on the stock of his rifle, Nick Dunn watched as Long Henry Thompson swung in closer to the chuck wagon belonging to the N Bar, the man's guttural voice loudly directing words at one of the cook's helpers. "You, dammit, Pierce, hump it with them taters. Dammit, bet you've slopped half of them outta that pan onto the ground, you clumsy ass—"

"Thompson," came the cook's jarring voice, "don't you be roustin' my help." It suddenly dawned on him, Jesse Snavely, a rotund man wearing a shapeless felt hat, that cowhand Henry Thompson wasn't sitting his saddle all that steadily. "Thompson, why, sure as hell you're drunk!"

"You son'bitch." Long Henry glared as he yanked out his Colt .45 and thumbed the hammer back. As he began leveling the barrel of his weapon on the chest of cook Snavely, the heavier, throttling roar of a rifle sounded, a leaden slug snatching Thompson's hat away.

Wheeling his horse around, Thompson cursed when he saw who it was that was holding the rifle, more curse words raining out at Nick Dunn. Now the drumming of hooves came from the direction of the herd ground, but this failed to register in the mind of Henry Thompson, who suddenly twisted in the saddle and fired his Colt. The cook folded down.

"Stampede!" The dreaded cry rang out even as Thompson was lashing his horse away from the campground and snatching a shot in the direction of Nick and others breaking toward their horses, which were pulling against halter ropes tied to the rope corral. The cowpokes were hefting saddles and pushing in amongst their horses, trying to work calmly over the gathering sound of the stampede. Someone cried out that the cattle were angling away from the campground to more open country, and a couple of shots rang out, distantly, probably a hand trying to turn the leaders.

Over by the chuck wagon some of the ranchers were standing over Tom Wilson where he knelt by the wounded cook. Tom had placed a towel over the wound to stem the flow of blood; but Snavely's face had gone ashen and he wasn't stirring around as much. Through the anger mottling his face rancher Wilber Farley said, "It was a damned cold-blooded act; that damned Long Henry."

"What d'ya think, Tom?"

Tom responded to Kelly Riggins's question by saying, "Nearest doctor is fifty miles away. Jesse's pulse is awful weak. Bring over some bedrolls an' we'll try to make 'im comfortable. Jesse, can you hear me?" They were old friends, going back to when Snavely had been a top hand before some serious injuries had put an end to that and he'd turned to cooking. Now he helped them lift Snavely onto a bedroll placed under the deeper shadow cast by the chuck wagon. Distantly to Tom came a rumbling sound of the herd still in full stampede, but out a ways now.

He said as he put a coverlet over Snavely, "The closest place is Galata . . . but that's still forty miles away." Tom Wilson straightened up and spotted a couple of hands about to pull out after the stampeding herd. "Hey you, Aston, an' Dunn, pull over here." He went to meet them as they cantered up close to the camp fire. "I want you boys to ride hard for Galata and fetch Doc Rickart. Tell 'im Jesse's got a bad chest wound. Now ride, boys."

No sooner had the two men pulled out to the north than ranchers Farley and Riggins, after conferring with Tom Wilson, were seeking their horses with the idea of helping to round up the cattle. As for Tom, the violence of what Thompson had done still hammered away at him. He should have followed his first instincts and not hired the gunhand. Too late now, he mused bitterly.

In a little less than an hour the cattle were brought under control and were beginning to settle down on the herd ground. A few steers had been killed, but fortunately no cowhands, though a horse had had the misfortune to snap a leg and had to be taken out of its misery. For the most part after this, everyone hung around the camp fires, their talk awfully quiet, and they began hitting their bedrolls around eleven, each man taking a squint at where cook Jesse Snavely was laid out by his chuck wagon. Their worst fears were realized just after midnight, and by then a lot were asleep and didn't learn until sunup that Snavely had cashed in his chips.

A grave was dug in the uncertain haze of morning, with everyone but those guarding the herd there to hear Tom Wilson and then Wilber Farley recite some Bible words. This wasn't a good start for the spring roundup, and everyone had this on his mind, along with a determination that if they ever ran across Long Henry Thompson they'd cut the man down. As they started to break away, waddy Clemet Hall picked out three shadowy forms pushing in hard from the north, a trio which turned out to be the sawbones from Galata and Dunn and Les Aston.

The pile of churned soil told them the sad yarn, and as the others sought their horses and began heading out to hunt up more cattle, Tom Wilson accompanied Doc Rickart and his two hands over to a chuck wagon, where they settled in around cups of coffee.

"Doc, seems Jesse wouldn't have lived anyway; that slug hit in too close to the heart. Mighty obliged you came, though."

"Tom," said Aston, "we didn't take the time to tell the law up there about this. But I figure Doc Rickart can tend to that when he gets back. A man with a temper like Thompson's will get plugged sooner or later. An' I hope it's sooner, dammit . . ."

"Know how you feel, Les," said Nick Dunn.

"You know, Nick," said Tom Wilson, "Long Henry'll want a piece of your hide for you usin' your rifle. But like Les just said, won't be long before he's probably taken out."

As Les Aston walked his bronc over to the horses still milling about in the rope corral, Dunn said, "How's Arte Reese farin'?"

"Appears you'll be the new wrangler, Nick. While you're here, Doc, maybe you could take a look at Arte?" The foreman walked with them over to where Les Aston had just snaked out a riata to hook it around the neck of a gelding, and he motioned

Arte Reese over, the man easing his horse in closer and swinging down.

Reese had a pained look on his face which was creased with deep lines and was ashen. He tried to stand up straighter, but it was an effort, and the waddy said encouragingly, "Just some back pain, Doc Rickart."

"Mind if I check you out?"

"Doggone it, Tom, I don't want nobody fussin' over me, I—"

"Last night, Arte, you never got a wink of sleep for the pain," replied Wilson. "There's a heap of days left to this spring roundup, and tendin' to the remuda is damned important. Doc'll check you out; now go along with him."

The foreman and Nick Dunn waited until Arte Reese was out of earshot, then Wilson said, "Arte just don't want to call it quits. And I think it's more than some back pains. Well, Nick, until otherwise, you're my day wrangler. Today we'll hold in here to brand what we've got, so just take the remuda out, probably along the river where the grass is thickest."

"Okay," Nick Dunn responded as Les Aston broke away to the southwest after some riders pushing over an elevation. Then, after unsaddling his spent horse, he roped another and put his rigging on its back. Now Nick broke down the rope corral to free the horses. As he rode after the remuda starting to drift west along the river, he looked back at the doctor, who was using his stethoscope on Arte Reese, the man's bare chest sticking out whitely against the worn side of the chuck wagon.

It didn't take him all that long to get the horses farther out to thicker grass, the bunch of over fifty broncs switching their tails and muzzling away at feeding themselves from the green grass shoots. By now, he surmised, the killing Henry Thompson was probably holed up at some cowtown nursing a bad hangover, but maybe not having any remorse about what he'd done. There was this feeling in Nick Dunn that their paths would cross again, and if so, only one of them would walk away.

THREE

By the time Henry Thompson reached Loma he couldn't recall the cook's last name, not that it mattered any. The two-day ride had flushed the whiskey out of his system, leaving him a little owlier, and the hunger pangs coming from his belly caused the rangy man to draw rein at a small cafe fringing the other business places. He tied the N Bar N bronc along the side wall as an old bulldog rumbled out from behind the building. Maybe it caught the scent of danger, or the smell coming from a man a long way between baths, but the dog growled its way behind the building again.

One thing that had stuck with Thompson was that if he ever saw this Nick Dunn again, there'd be a showdown. He should have killed Dunn instead of that cook back there, but his head hadn't been on right. He was going to quit anyway, and it sure would have helped to have his back pay; but what the hell, Loma had a bank. The cowtown lay south along the Marias River, northeast some twenty-five miles from Fort Benton. He'd bypass the fort when he took off for Sand Coulee, where Thompson hoped to make contact with some men he'd ridden with before. "Well, I'm broke . . . but damned if I'm goin' hungry 'cause of that." And somewhat tiredly he found the front door of the Hayrack Cafe.

He sank into a front booth so that he could survey the customers, his looming presence coming as it had out of the morning sun bringing a lot of questioning stares to him. For a while he simply eyeballed the locals back, and buffaloed, they got back to the business of exchanging gossip. The waitress coming to take his order wasn't half bad, a little plump but she had a wiggle to her walk, and she returned his tired smile. "The works," he simply said. "And first, a pot of Arbuckles to chase the trail dust away."

When she came back with a fresh pot of coffee he inquired about the local law, learning that town marshal Clemens had taken the stage down to White Sulphur Springs to enjoy the mineral springs. Vaguely he recalled the marshal's first name, and he said pleasantly, "Dan Clemens, wasn't he a deputy sheriff one time?"

"Few years back he was. Don't need much law over here, which is why they gave him the job." She left a reluctant smile behind as a customer called out he needed a refill. Her name was Loraine Carson, and she liked rough-hewn men, which fit the stranger right down to his bold eyes.

Henry Thompson didn't waste any time when the waitress came back with his food, and he asked her straight out, "You live here, I expect . . ."

"Not all that long. Was waitressing up at Virgelle until six months ago. Been here ever since. I . . . I got a room over at the Farragut Hotel. Why'd you ask, Mister—?"

"Ah, Ed Larkin. Thought you might like some company tonight." He began sprinkling pepper over the eggs and biscuits and gravy. Henry Thompson saw no need to pay for a hotel room when other lodging was available, in this case Loraine, as she told him this and, yes, tonight would be fine.

"Loraine, fellow I worked for is comin' inta town today to pay me off; maybe you could put this on the cuff 'til then?"

"No problem, Ed."

"Obliged," came his easy response, and when she went back to wait on other customers, the cold glitter pierced back into Henry Thompson's eyes.

After a second plate of food, the gunhand left to walk his bronc downstreet toward a livery stable, burping contentedly as he ambled along. Farther along the street there was another livery stable, and this side of that stood about fifteen buildings making up Loma's business sector. The town looked like it had weathered a hard winter, in that most of the frame buildings could use a coat of paint. And some of them were empty, a common sight in places like this. There were only a handful of saddled horses tethered along the street, and some buggies, and during spring roundup the town would stay quiet until cowhands came whooping in again to chase the elephant.

Pleasing Thompson was the appearance of the Stockman's Bank, where it stood on the corner next to a saddlery shop. In passing the bank he took in the name of the banker in gilded letters on the closed door, along with the hours the bank was open for business. The way these western banks operated, he knew, was by giving out ranch loans. During hard times if a rancher went under, the bank would foreclose, and then set somebody up to manage the ranch they now owned. He'd bet that a good many ranches up in these parts were run that way, meaning that Long Henry put all bankers into one greedy pot.

Through the open livery door Thompson walked the bronc. He tied the reins to a stall post as a man trundled a wheelbarrow in through the back door and nodded his head at the stranger. "Be with you in a minute."

Looking about, Henry Thompson eyed the horses in the stalls, in particular a bay that showed plenty of bottom. It was a big horse, nearly thirteen hands high, he reckoned, and as he was a big man, he knew he'd be forking that bay out of here. He turned to the chore of unsaddling the bronc.

"How's Tom Wilson?"

Masking his surprise, Thompson smiled back at the hostler while using a checkered bandanna to wipe the sweat from his face. "Still segundo out at the N Bar. When does the stage pull out for Great Falls?"

"Won't come through until day after tomorrow. Why'd you ask?"

"Aim to take it to Miles City," he lied. "My pa passed away, and I've got to get back there to settle the estate before those lawyers and bankers steal it all, if you know what I mean. Bought this here bronc, but forkin' it all the way to Miles City . . . just too far . . ."

"So you want to sell it." The hostler checked the bay's teeth, and then worked his way along the side of the horse, poking as he went to check muscle tone and so on. Both of them knew the horse was sound; the hostler's edge was that maybe this cowpoke wasn't up on market price. "In good shape."

"I won't haggle with you," the gunhand said. "I ride that hoss down to Great Falls, I could probably get eighty to a hundred for it. So what say you offer me sixty for it."

"Tolerable price."

"Downstreet there's another livery stable," he cautioned.

"You keepin' the saddle and riggin'?" At Thompson's nod, the hostler added, "Okay, sixty it is; and cash money, I expect." They both laughed at this. He led the way into his booth of an office, where from a cigar box he took out some rumpled bills and counted into Thompson's large hand sixty in greenbacks. The gunhand was out the door and halfway up the street before the hostler realized he hadn't asked for a bill of sale. He shrugged this away, knowing he would make a profit on the bronc, and then he was back at the task of shoveling horse droppings into his wheelbarrow.

Maybe it was because the wind came roaring through these parts a lot that the saloon Henry Thompson had decided to check out was called The Creaking Door Bar. Long ago he'd decided he disliked wind maybe more'n smart-ass cooks and other riffraff. Being bigger than most, he found it sport to goad someone loaded down with whiskey into a fight, or he'd even buy the drinks just to get a man into that condition, and then Thompson's rocklike fists would play a tattoo on his victim's face. Thinking on it, he figured he got this mean streak from his grandma's side of the family. He knew of at least two that Lydia Mae Turpin had taken out before she'd died of consumption and other complications at age ninety-one. He didn't figure on, nor was he particularly concerned about, living that long.

"A mean ol' bitch," he muttered as his wide shoulders pushed the batwings aside. Back in the dimness of a hallway a swamper was yielding a broom, and at a table one old gent was just sitting there and mumbling to himself over a cup of coffee. The barroom had a low ceiling, and Thompson looked bigger than life standing there, as the crown of his brown Stetson rode just below the dark yellow-enameled ceiling. Then he noticed the ceiling rose some as it spilled on toward the back wall. The man presiding over the barroom turned idly away from the potbellied stove where he was pouring himself some coffee, and he said, "Yup, we're open." The light in here wasn't all that good as the windows were caked over with a film of dust, and he squinted his way back behind the bar.

But there was enough light for Long Henry Thompson to determine he knew this rotund gent, and yeah, from down south of here in Colorado. Going up to the bar, he mumbled out he wanted a whiskey and chaser. He flopped down a worn greenback, which the barkeep picked up and began making change. "You just ridin' through?"

"Depends. I don't suppose you heard, but Ducky Medrick got hung down in Taos."

"Mister, just who the hell is . . ."

"If you ain't Buck 'Sixtoes' Baker, I'm a damned sheepherder."

The barkeep's eyes lost their disinterested squint. "Yeah, it's you, Henry Thompson," he muttered quietly while checking to see they weren't being overheard. "Here I'm known as Buck Green; and I'd like to keep it that way."

"Won't be me ratting on you, Buck. Fact is, I'm short on cash and just passin' through on my way down to Shonkin. Which is where you come in."

"That so?" he questioned warily. He knew Long Henry well enough not to provoke the man into an argument or otherwise make him get all fired up. Shonkin, a small watering hole shaded by Highwood Peak just to the south, was where men on the dodge would come, to pick up messages or drop one off. "Look, Henry, I just work here, so I could only loan you a sawbuck or two . . ."

"No, ain't lookin' for loose change, Buck." He emptied his glass to have it filled with whiskey again. "We're the same in that we don't like cold weather all that much. Wouldn't be here if so many damned starpackers weren't lookin' for us down south."

"Yup," he agreed, "I know of at least five more we rode with before scattered around up here. Doin' odd jobs like me until somethin' turns up."

"Something has," said Thompson. "An' in your line of work."

Interest flared on Buck Baker's pockmarked face. He poured a little whiskey into his coffee cup, and looked to make sure the swamper wasn't in hearing distance. "You've always been particular about who you rode with. So just who is comin' into Shonkin—"

"Black Jack Christian and his High Fives bunch. Like us, Arizona got too hot for them." Thompson smiled back in the knowledge that Buck Sixtoes Baker would hook up with them. It was just a stroke of luck him pulling in here to run into Baker, probably the best brand burner he'd ever known. "Black Jack'll fill me in on the particulars. Meanin' his connections up here. The word I got is big money's involved. And speakin' of dinero, Buck, tell me about your local banker."

"Name's Cyrus Spurgeon; son'bitch is awful tight with loanin' out money. He'll do so if you don't need it. But you want to know about his bad habits, yup, Spurgeon got some of those same's us—gambling, can't hold his liquor worth a damn, and maybe others hidden in his closet. Tonight, as a matter of fact, he'll be sittin' in this high stakes game upstreet at the Blue Moon casino."

"I'll wrangle an invite into the game," said Thompson. "You interested in hookin' up with me and the High Fives?"

"If you boys'll have me."

"Okay, Buck, here's what I want you to do."

One of the things Henry Thompson had done in mid-afternoon was to call upon banker Cyrus Spurgeon, where he had the banker close the door to his office before Thompson opened a small doeskin pouch and spilled out some gold nuggets. They were small, and there was some leaf gold, too. Henry Thompson explained that his mining partner was due in most any time. Actually he'd gotten the gold from Sixtoes Baker, just a sampling amounting to around a hundred dollars, but enough to arouse the banker's greedy curiosity. The deal they'd struck was that if Thompson's partner showed that evening, the banker would let them store their gold in his big Ferguson vault. Out of this Thompson had also wrangled an invitation into tonight's high stakes poker game.

Since sundown he had been squiring waitress Loraine Carson around the saloons, having picked her up at her hotel, where she'd allowed him to stash his saddle rigging and possible sack in her room. He hadn't been at all surprised at the offer to partake of the whiskey bottle reposing on the dresser. After which they'd snuggled under the covers to make love. Now, as eight o'clock tolled and the mercantile stores were locking their front doors, he was ushering Loraine into the Blue Moon casino.

The casino, he found, was awfully lavish for being located in an out-of-the-way cowtown like Loma. He picked up on the scent of new paint, and along with this, there was a U-shaped balcony above the main barroom. Where the U opened, velvety blue curtains were strung across a wide stage, and there were plenty of tables for the customers idling at them to watch the show now in progress, that of two cowboy types strumming on guitars and singing lustily their plaintive rendition of the "Last Roundup." During the day Loma had seemed like a ghost town, and Henry Thompson had the notion the people crowding the barroom must have crawled out of the woodwork. He felt right at home.

He brought Loraine over to one of the few empty tables, noticing she was one of the few women in the casino, as he'd discounted the bar girls and the whores. As soon as they were comfortable, she latched on to his arm, snuggled in close and batted her cow-sick eyes at him as if they were engaged. Not only had she provided him with a free room, but being with her had made Thompson halfway acceptable to the locals.

"Ma'am," he said to the bar girl. "Whiskey for me and the lady—and a round for the house."

"Oh, Ed," Loraine Carson gushed, "why, drinks around'll set you back a pretty penny."

"I expect to get it back in that poker game." He nodded to where banker Spurgeon was sitting with some gentlemen friends. "Our Mr. Spurgeon is sure putting the rotgut away; an' from what I learned he can't hold the stuff all that good. And speakin' of good, feel mighty fine inside, woman."

"Anybody got any requests?" asked the performers on stage.

"Yeah, I got one," called out a leather-lunged drinker to the musicians. "There's a stage leavin' for Helena at midnight—be under it!" Guffaws drowned out the babble of talk.

Chastened, but still determined, the duo strummed into an oldie, "A Bird in a Gilded Cage." Then an empty whiskey bottle sailed its way to crash down on the stage, and a bouncer immediately latched on to the bottle thrower to more guffaws. Henry Thompson looked up and returned the smile of the banker, who was now standing beside him.

"I see, Mr. Larkin, you did accept my invitation to join our little game."

"Just hope it was the wise thing to do, sir." He turned his head and whispered to his table companion, "Honey, won't take me all that long to shear these local yokels. Soon's I'm done I'll come to your room . . . and that's all right . . ."

"Oh, Ed, you know I'll be there, sugah. Don't be all night."

He rose and followed the banker down along a back hallway,

knowing he'd never set his eyes on the waitress again, and
scarcely remembering what she looked like. Long Henry had
planted his seed throughout the West in the fifteen years he'd
been a gunfighter, and never had looked back or cared all that
much. In his opinion it took two to tango. He wondered what
he would do if someone came up and called him Daddy . . .
probably gun the result of his long-ago indiscretion down.

Two hours into the game, Henry Thompson was five hundred
ahead and starting another deal. The game was a big one, seated
to the limit with seven players, and there wasn't much small
talk. Part of this, as Long Henry had figured out, was that it
seemed everyone there but him was in hock to Cyrus Spurgeon's
Stockman's Bank. They were cordial but not overly friendly to
the banker, but would damn sure crack a smile or laugh when
Spurgeon told a joke. At times, when he was the only one bucking heads with the banker, Thompson would fold his cards and
let the man rake in the pot. Drunkenly Spurgeon would flail his
arms and chuckle around a greedy smile as he scooped in the
chips. What he never did was offer to buy a round of drinks,
which Thompson had, and the others, and the gunfighter was
getting sick of sitting across the table from the banker.

After shuffling the deck, he set the cards over to be cut,
and as he began dealing out the pasteboards, the bar girl who'd
been feeding them drinks reappeared and sought out Henry
Thompson, then handed him a folded piece of paper. Scribbled
there, he found a message from his cohort, Sixtoes Baker, and
he shaped a smile for banker Spurgeon.

"My partner just pulled into town, I'm pleased to announce.
Gal, bring drinks around . . . as doggone it, Mr. Spurgeon,
I . . ."

"Now, now," cautioned the banker, "that'll be our little se-
cret. You boys go on with the game while Mr. Larkin and I
conduct a little business." He weaved up from the chair.
"Won't be long now . . . so don't fret none."

They left the room and went out the back door, and it wasn't
long, less than five minutes, before Cyrus Spurgeon was fum-

bling a key into the lock of the front door. It was a shade after midnight, and Main Street showed some movement; but nobody seemed to notice the two of them slipping into the bank. Thompson said, "My partner'll be waitin' out back . . ."

"With all that gold," said the banker as he pushed in past the teller cages and into the office area of his small bank. "You know, Mr. Larkin, I can invest some of your gold in various companies on the Stock Exchange. Right now . . . yes, I'd better unlock the back door. You said you boys collected at least three hundred thousand in gold nuggets . . ." Opening the back door, he gazed out at the shadowy figure standing by a pair of saddled horses; there was a third horse and it appeared to be loaded down with packs.

"I'll give Ol' Zephraim a hand while you open the vault," suggested Thompson as he stepped outside, with the banker nodding in befuddlement and going back up toward the wall vault.

Spurgeon worked the combination dial, his anxious fingers finally getting the door to unlatch, and he was swinging it wide open when the creak of floorboards announced the arrival of the miners and this bonanza in gold nuggets. Cruelly Thompson slugged the man over the crown of his head with the butt of his Colt .45. Thompson said surly, "Don't have to listen to that mealy-mouthed banker again. Okay, Sixtoes, let's sack up the money and beeline out of this lemon-suckin' burg."

"That Loraine, I didn't treat her all that rough when I went up there to fetch your stuff, Henry. What threw me, though, was when that door opened she was naked as a jaybird. Clothes do hide a lot of things, I found out."

"Just so you left her bound and gagged is all I care."

And when they pulled out within the half-hour, they left the banker stretched out in his own vault. Boldly they stuck to the main stagecoach road instead of trying to pick their way south along the Sun River. Even though he intended to keep them saddlebound for the rest of the night, Henry Thompson was satisfied. He was riding a stolen horse and had a heap of stolen money in his possession. And probably had sired another frontier brat.

"Yup, Sixtoes, it'll feel good to hook up with the High Fives again."

"They got some big plans, which pleases me no end." Twisting back, Sixtoes pulled a whiskey bottle out of a saddlebag as they jogged along under starlight. "Here, I cleaned out the bar's prime stuff."

Laughing, Thompson said, "That'll help chase away these moonlight blues. Yup, Sixtoes, we've got some big killing plans. Only it won't be this blue cheese color, but blood red, that ol' moon'll be beaming down upon . . . blood of whoever's stupid enough to get in our way . . ."

FOUR

Ten days into the roundup found everyone, and that included the horses, falling into the daily routine of shagging out before sunup and going after more cattle. As set out early on, they were working their way west over a wide swath of land claimed by the ranchers participating in the roundup, and it would be at least another four or five days before they'd encounter men from the Shelby roundup.

The long, saddlebound days began with the cooks rousting the hands out around three in the morning, and after a hasty breakfast of Arbuckles, fat pork, biscuits, and beans, the captain of the roundup, Tom Wilson, would sing out: "All right, boys, catch your hosses!"

Since hovering near the warm-up fire might cause them to spend the day afoot, they hurried over to where the night wrangler was driving the saddle band into a rope corral rigged up by stretching some ropes between the wheels of the mess and bedroll wagons and across to square it out by some trees. One of the best ropers, Cal Kincaid of the W Slash F, had been picked to do the morning roping, and he lassoed at the discretion of each waddy a particular horse, which the cowpoke then walked out of the corral and set about cinching the saddle into place. In a little while, some fifty cowhands awaited orders from the captain, who was slouched in his saddle amongst the ranchers, while a dozen or so other cowhands had pulled out to drive the day herd to the new camping ground.

Along with all of this responsibility, one of Tom Wilson's wisdom teeth had started to ache something fierce, and about all he had to ease the pain were some cloves a cook had given him. Quickly, though, he divided the men into two bands. "Kelly," he said to rancher Kelly Riggins, "you take this bunch and work about fifteen miles out on this side of the Teton. And, Murdock, take the others thataway. Branding camp'll be on the Teton near Lost Butte." And then Wilson set out along the ruts left by the departing wagons, with tallyman Wyman Pruitt as his riding companion. At the new campsite he would preside over the branding crew and be there when cattle were brought in.

"Another long day," commented the tallyman.

"A lot more of them to come, Wyman."

"Been wonderin' if anybody's caught up to Henry Thompson . . ."

"Once roundup is over," Tom said bitterly, "me and everyone else will be out gunning for Long Henry—man did what he did doesn't even deserve a decent burial."

Farther to the northwest another member of the roundup was also thinking about the murder committed by Long Henry Thompson. Nick Dunn was lazing the remuda along, but generally letting the horses pull up to graze when they came to taller grass. The suddenness of the killing had made Dunn realize if he ever encountered Thompson, there'd be no angry words exchanged before they unleathered their sidearms. A man would be wiser to take Thompson out in an ambush, a notion that was maybe cowardly but would at least guarantee him staying alive.

In him, too, were thoughts about Wyoming. Of Buffalo and Sheridan and the Big Horns. Of certain lawmen he knew, and the hope that some of them were dead by now. Nick was toying with the idea that perhaps it would be better to find a nice bank in some quiet cowtown and, after robbing it, head out to Seattle and catch a South American bound ship. At least down there he wouldn't have to be watching his back trail all the time. Though ever since settling in here with the N Bar, he'd relaxed more, especially with the departure of Henry Thompson.

Yesterday two more ranchers had hooked up to what they called the Box Elder roundup, since this was where most of these cattlemen went to buy supplies and socialize. And for Nick the additional men meant adding a heap more saddle mounts to the remuda. He hadn't minded all that much as he loved and understood horses. Sometimes a horse was a man's best friend, the mount keeping him a couple of days ahead of some posse. He had taken to studying the remuda, getting to know the animals much like a mother cow knows her calf. As Nick hazed them from camp to camp on this roundup, a mental picture began emerging as to each horse's characteristics and habits. By doing this he was able to control them by his own brains and not the speed of the horse he rode.

Late yesterday afternoon, to Nick's dismay, a bunch quitter had cut away to make a break for its home range, forcing Nick to ride the hocks off his horse, but he'd caught the breakaway and come riding in that night with a complete remuda. But if that horse had gotten away, he'd have sure caught living hell from Tom Wilson. As a matter of fact, Wilson had been making a count each day of the remuda, watching closely to see if Nick was up to being wrangler, and early this morning, shortly after both of them had got up, there'd been a quiet word of praise from Tom Wilson. Tonight Nick would welcome turning the remuda over to the nighthawk, for he liked jawing away with his newfound friends, Aston and Hall and others, before they all climbed into their bedrolls, hoping once again it would be a quiet night.

"Hiyeee," Nick called out as he cut over sharply on his horse to go after some mounts that had strayed out too far from the main bunch. Once the horses were lazing back in closer, he reined up and hooked a leg over the saddle horn and slouched as he took out the makings. "Boring as hell out here . . . but at least I ain't gettin' shot at . . ."

* * *

The guitar-playing Les Aston was in the bunch holding about five miles south of the river. This morning he was mounted on a grulla he'd named Lonesome Joe, since the bronc liked nothing better than getting rid of its rider and making tracks to where it could be alone, but other than this it gave Aston little trouble. The morning work was called circle riding, meaning that as his riders went out, Kelly Riggins would detach men from time to time to have them search certain sections of the range for cattle, until finally those farthest away came in searching on lines that tended to a common center as of an open fan.

After Aston had dropped away with Stope Marshall, a 77 hand, as his partner, they began searching between soapstone buttes for cattle, in pockets, basins, and coulees, which were covered with dense patches of brushwood or wind-beaten trees. It was dark but getting onto first light when they began scaring up cattle, and to the bawling of cows and calves they began hazing them north toward the Teton. Out here they had still to put in fence lines, and the hands found as the morning progressed the cattle they were gathering came from different ranches and had mingled together over the long winter: longhorns, shorthorn bulls and angus and white faces.

They simply let the cattle keep drifting along as they searched behind, now with Aston pushing his bronc into a lowering draw choked with brush, the softer ground signalling the presence of water. He scared out some cattle, less than half a dozen, and then by a creek he pulled up hard to take in the remnants of a large camp fire. Markings around it told of several horses being held here, and he knew that if the fire had been made last fall, the long winter would have erased signs of it.

He got down, reminded of a conversation he'd overheard between Tom Wilson and a few others just the other day, that the word was out rustlers had been working this part of northern Montana, and until a tally was made, none of the ranchers could ascertain their personal losses. Ground hitching the reins, he worked his way closer to the creek where he came across the drying hoof marks left by cattle.

"Not all that old . . . a week or two . . ."

Gazing across the creek, he could see where the cattle had been driven across. No doubt on this side they had been held in a rope corral while brand blotters went to work. The first rays of the sun struck down at him and along the creek, to glint off of something, which upon closer inspection turned out to be an empty can. There'd be other debris, he knew. He pushed through some low bushes and found other discarded cans and whiskey bottles, and then Les Aston struck pay dirt.

With his gloved hand he pushed a bush aside and picked up a running iron as he exclaimed, "Haven't seen one of these things in a heap of years."

The iron he held was made in the form of a straight poker curved at the end and used, he knew, much like the free style of writing on a blackboard with chalk. In the Seventies, Texas had passed a law, as did other western states, banning its use. This was a blow aimed at the brand blotter, whose innocent single iron didn't tell no tales if he was caught riding across the range with it tied to his saddle. The law made the man found with a single running iron an object of suspicion, and he was sometimes obliged to explain to a mighty urgent jury.

Going back to his horse, Aston climbed into the saddle and loped it back out of the draw, where his whistle caused his cow-hunting partner to rein up and wait for him. He handed the running iron to Stope Marshall and explained where he'd found it. "Times," drawled Stope, "have changed when it comes to blotting out brands."

What he meant was that the rustler had found he could use a cinch ring by heating it and holding it between two pliable sticks such as green twigs from trees. Also, the tool was easy to hide in his saddle lining or some other convenient place. The best rustling gambit, though, was that of using a telegraph wire or baling wire to make a better brand. These wires could be curved into any shape and could be quickly folded and hidden in a small place, after making a brand that easily melted into the scars of the cow's present brand. The clever rustler bent his wire so that the new mark it made would simply be an addition to the old lines. The only way to prove that this had been done was to skin the animal and read the inside of the hide.

They forked ahead, Aston tying the running iron to his saddle, on toward rising dust and a treeline marking the river. They'd scared up around a hundred head and were bringing the cattle in slowly while keeping a careful eye on the calves as some appeared to be only hours old. Pushing the cattle over an elevation, Aston could make out in the east a couple of miles the day wrangler, Nick Dunn, keeping watch over the remuda. Away to the north and across the narrow ribbon of river a few more dust columns tainted the midmorning sky. It still felt good to Les Aston to be working cattle after idling down south during the winter. The processes of summer put weight on the cattle; yet they worked differently for men like Aston, in that come autumn he'd be leaned out. He let Marshall take care of getting the small bunch of cattle over to the main herd as Aston cut around to the left and toward the main campsite.

The first man to nod in recognition was Wyman Pruitt, who was writing something in his tally book, and interest flared in Pruitt's eyes when he watched Aston untie the running iron from the back of his saddle, while bossman Tom Wilson rode over. He handed the iron to Tom, who studied it while listening to Aston narrate just how he'd found it.

Tom said, "I was hoping they were just rumors, rustlers working up here. Down thataway, land owned by Gene Downey. Gene went with Kelly's bunch this morning . . . and he won't be too happy about this." He laid his eyes on a "ketch hand" dragging a calf up to be branded and castrated, the flankers darting in to pin the calf down.

"Hot iron," one of the men holding the calf yelled, "W Slash F brand." Now the iron man picked out a branding iron bearing that particular brand from the red-hot coals of the fire and came over, but before applying the iron to the flank of the calf, he hit the rod against his forearm to jar away a few clinging embers of coal. There was a short hiss and the scent of burning hair, a doleful wail of agony and fear issuing from the calf. When released, the calf struggled to its clumsy legs and trotted off to seek its mother and sympathy.

That Tom Wilson was disturbed over the news and the running iron brought to him by Aston revealed itself in the tightening of his jaw muscles as he and Aston rode their horses over to dismount by a chuck wagon. He hated thievery in any form. It was Tom's old-fashioned credo that if a man wanted something he oughtta work to get it. Stealing cattle or horses was the same as stealing a lifetime of hard work from a man, for there were many former cowpunchers out here who'd started up small, hardscrabble ranches and were just barely hanging on. Their credentials were based on honesty, and if one of them agreed to something, a handshake sealed the bargain; and a man would rather die or go under than break his word. "Rustling," he spat out distastefully as the cook handed them tin cups, which threw heat through the gloves they wore.

Tipping his hat back, Les Aston said, "Hope this doesn't put a damper on this roundup."

"Biggest one we've had in years. It isn't like this hasn't happened before, Les. Hosses or cattle roaming free out here are always tempting targets to high line riders. They'll get together a small bunch, hoping to find a market for them someplace—then these thievin' suckers find a place to hole up until their dinero runs out."

"You think," speculated Aston, "Henry Thompson could be involved in this?"

"Dunno, as he's more the gunfighter type. Usin' a running iron or swinging a riata could do damage to his hands and slow his draw down. Thompson"—Tom Wilson frowned ponderingly—"went south for two, three years. Then he came back."

"Probably 'cause things got too hot for him down there."

"Yeah, probably. Well, Les, you and Stope, after he's gulped down that java, better head out and push out more cattle. Turned into a nice day." He had a smile for the pair of cowpunchers setting their cups in the washtub perched on the tailgate of the chuck wagon. And then Tom Wilson did the same thing, and swung back into the saddle and rode back to oversee branding operations.

When he got up to Wyman Pruitt, he asked, "How's the tally going?"

"Hot and heavy, Tom. The calfs look like they weathered the rigors of spring all right . . . though some of them are just a bag of skin and bones."

"We'll have to get word to the stock inspector over at Shelby," he said in reference to the running iron he'd left on the chuck wagon.

"That'll be Poul Gregson—a good man."

W.D. "Billy" Smith, chief stock inspector of the Montana Stockman's Association, had just made one of his rare trips to Shelby. He was stationed way to the east at Miles City now, chiefly due to the flurry of rustling taking place in the Badlands abutting the eastern fringes of Montana. The rustling had gotten so bad it had forced some ranchers into bankruptcy.

What hurt more than anything was his arriving here in Shelby the day after Poul Gregson had died as a result of being hit with a slug from a Winchester rifle. Billy Smith and the sheriff of Cole County and a handful of others made up those who'd followed the hearse out here to this oak-shaded cemetery. Stock Inspector Gregson had lingered on for several days, but he'd been in a coma, and the details of the shooting had been given to Billy Smith by the sheriff, just some fuzzy details of how Poul had stumbled into the camp of some rustlers.

The warming wind of early summer ruffling around him, Billy Smith tossed the small clod of dirt he was holding onto the pine coffin. He put on his gray Stetson and fell into step with Sheriff Ira Clark. "I hear," said Clark, "that rustling is really bad over your way."

"An epidemic; just hope it doesn't spread into these parts. Poul, too bad he couldn't have given us a better description of these men."

"He rambled on a lot. Could be three men, or three times that number of rustlers. The cowhands who found Poul Gregson out there said there'd been one helluva rainstorm about that time. Time I got out to where Poul'd been shot, the trail of whoever did this was wiped out. I figure he was shot around sundown or shortly thereafter . . . otherwise he wouldn't have got as far as he did. So, Billy, where does that leave us?"

"Me to look for someone to replace Poul. Something I'll have to take up with the stockman's committee."

"What I have in mind, Billy, is to get together with some other county sheriffs and compare notes. It would be helpful to know who these killers are. It could be the Hayward gang, or even that Miller bunch from over Colstrip way." They got into the sheriff's buggy; then he headed back into town.

Astride a rented horse and sitting in a saddle that he had trouble getting used to, W.D. Smith continued on through rugged prairie where the next cowtown lay at least another hundred miles to the east. He was following directions given him by the sheriff, and had left shortly after the sheriff had dropped him off at the livery stable. His reason for coming out here was that two of the ranchers participating in the Shelby roundup were on the executive committee of the stockman's association that controlled this part of the state. And through them he hoped to hire a man to take over for the dead Poul Gregson, who'd been a pretty good cowhand before becoming a stock detective.

Another thing the sheriff had told him was of the ranchers from farther east of here also pooling together to form the Box Elder roundup bunch. The two groups would eventually run into one another out here, but gazing into the hazy distance, Billy Smith knew this might not happen until a week or two down the line.

"Gotta get back to Miles City and hire some more stock detectives. Or a lot more ranchers back there'll be goin' under 'cause of this intolerable rustling."

Back at Shelby, his thoughts continued, the sheriff had mentioned the Miller gang headed up by aging Red Miller, about the meanest son'bitch in these parts. And, yeah, the Haywards, some newcomers, as he'd never heard of them before. But like the sheriff said, too, the outlaw trail pushing up along the Rockies wasn't all that far away. The perfect route for more high liners to come in and latch on to some cattle and get out faster than a lightning bug. Instead of one, he'd have to urge these ranchers to take on two if not more stock detectives. For if you quelled this rustling right away, and let the newspapers and outlaws get wind of it, they'd think twice before coming in here to Montana. Should have done this back in eastern Montana, he'd kept harping at the Stockman's Association bigwheels, but like most with money, they hated to part with more if they could get by cheaply.

"All this travelin' I've been doin'," he lamented, "oughtta drag in more salary . . . but to see the sour looks on their faces whenever I do . . ."

Distantly, to the southeast, he spotted dust being fanned away by the wind, and it took him a while—after his horse had covered nearly a quarter of a mile—before he could discern cattle being pushed along by cowpokes. By his reckonings, it would be late afternoon before he'd reach the main herd, probably being held out in more open ground, and where there was a creek to keep the cattle from going dry as the branding went on.

And so Billy Smith let himself drift inwardly to muse over

those wanteds he had stuffed into his saddlebag. Prominent among them was one on Starky True. Though True hadn't committed any crimes in Montana, at least none they were aware of, Wyoming lawmen had sent word to be on the lookout for the gunman. Or maybe not, as Billy Smith recalled a recent chat he'd had in Big Timber, when he'd been passing through and the stage had stopped to exchange horses. The town marshal there had told him that he was damned positive Starky True had been spotted down in Waco, and not all that long ago.

"Hope so, as it's one less I have to worry about."

With the sun at his back, Billy Smith stared past his elongating shadow at the beckoning lights of camp fires and the large herd of cattle holding south of a creek. They were still branding calfs, and now he turned his head to see another small bunch of cattle being hazed in.

He held up, to breathe his horse, and to watch a scene out of his own cowboying past, with silent envy choking in his throat. Even through the dust that was swirling about the branding fires and out amongst the cattle, he saw that most of the cattle bore Ollie Knudsen's Circle K brand, as this was part of Knudsen's ranch. After being branded, the main herd except for cattle bearing other brands would be hazed away from the creek and turned loose.

Back and forth through this dust those on cutting horses swung and charged, swooping wide to round in a galloping steer, flinging their sweating horses at the congested herd. Calves lumbered awkwardly in a halfhearted gallop after their mothers, their tongues hanging from the sides of their mouths and dribbling with a lathery foam. Here and there some mother cow with a heaving of ribs and flanks would bust into a long-drawn bawl rising for an instant to a high pitch and ending in a throaty rumble. All of this bawling and bellering, the crackling of horns and pounding of hooves, along with the dusty whirl of worried cattle was, Billy Smith reminisced, a part of the roundup. Adding to this were the shrill yells and yips of the cowpokes, to Smith's ears a mighty savage music.

Not all that many cowhands were allowed to cut out from the herd, since too many riders at once got the cattle stirred up, and cows and calves got separated from each other. This cutting out called for bold and skillful riding and involved considerable personal danger. It was hard, wearing work, keeping both rider and horse constantly on the alert. The cowpokes did this slowly as speed in this game didn't save time.

Itching to get in for some coffee to chase the dust out of his throat and to see old friends, Billy Smith spurred the gelding on, though he knew he was bringing unpleasant news. What Smith hadn't been informed of, as word still hadn't gotten to Shelby, was about Long Henry Thompson adding another notch to his sixgun, this when the gunfighter had gunned down that N Bar N cook. He would learn about this when he returned to Shelby, and also about the bank robbery over at Loma. Later on Billy Smith would come to realize these unconnected events were a prelude to what came to be known in these parts as, "The Killing Summer." But for now there was the job of unloading to these men involved in the Shelby roundup the sad news of Pool Gregson's untimely death at the hands of rustlers.

"Evening, Mr. Knudsen, and howdy, Kyle Rote."

Ollie Knudsen, a big, solemn-faced Norse, said, "W.D., whenever you show up, there's been trouble someplace—"

"So, Billy, better spill it out first," enjoined Rote.

"Reckon you boys are right," said Billy Smith, as he was only so grateful to vacate the saddle. "This won't be easy, but here's the shank of it . . ."

FIVE

There was nothing better than showing up with your saddlebags bulged out by greenbacks, and with some old friends to help spend your ill-begotten riches. And Shonkin was a place where an owlhoot could have a good time, no lawman to hassle them and plenty of whiskey near at hand and some willing women. Henry Thompson and Sixtoes Baker didn't mind sharing their money with the High Fives gang, since the shadowy plan outlined to them by gang leader Black Jack Christian would gain them a lot more than they'd taken from the bank in Loma.

Shonkin had three saloons and not much else, and though a cowhand would come in from time to time, he wouldn't hang around long for fear of getting slipped a "Mickey Finn" and rolled. And if this didn't befall him, chances were he'd lose his money in a crooked card game. It was here a U.S. marshal or some posse would come looking for men on the dodge. Despite this, the small scattering of buildings were a haven, and more, a place to pick up on where some old owlhoot buddies were hiding out.

Wherein Long Henry got his name because of his size, it was Burt Christian's love for playing Black Jack that had gotten this moniker hung on him. At five-eleven, he was a couple of inches shorter than Thompson, but lean, and with one of those frames that shed away gainful pounds no matter how much he ate, which at times was considerable. He was a pure-quill killer; eleven had died by his hand. He had sandy hair and light blue eyes, and could think clearly when that was needed. Like now, Black Jack considered all the angles before he undertook something.

The saloon the outlaws were presently in, as they had drank the others dry, was really an old hip-roofed barn that a half-hearted carpenter had shaped into a barroom. Some rough planking covered the dirt floor where the cows and horses had once shed their manure, and after all the stalls had been taken out, a bar had been made and tables and chairs put in; but the old stench still remained to some extent. A rickety staircase led up to the hayloft divided into pine-board rooms. Now that the High Fives were holding in here, all of the whores from the other saloons had drifted over. The God of the demimonde was coin of the realm, the silver dollar.

From where he sat, Thompson let all of what he'd just absorbed push through his mind. What it was was a rustling operation backed up by Montana money men, or otherwise sly Black Jack Christian wouldn't have bought in. Part of it also involved the stockman's association, and this was what had puzzled Long Henry. He said, "Those stock detectives are a heap more honest than town marshals or sheriffs."

"My man in Havre is gonna handle that."

"Your man in Havre, huh? The town drunk, I suppose."

Black Jack's smile widened, for he knew how cynical Thompson could get at times. But he needed the man, since Thompson knew the country up here. "Look, Henry, everything's in place. You'll get a fair share out of what we make."

"You can count me in," Thompson muttered. He looked past Black Jack at the rest of the outlaws sitting at tables, and he felt a little better about agreeing to join them. They were all old hands at an assortment of crimes, the dead giveaway they'd just arrived from a warmer climate their deeper-tanned faces. There was Black Jack's older brother, Will, a man without too much ambition, but steady in a gunfight. And Bob Hays, a black man and probably the best bronc buster he'd ever seen. The sullen one, and the only outlaw without a whore draped all over him, was George Musgrove, who was once, would you believe it, a preacher. Musgrove would have these dark spells, at which time anything could happen, and often did. The money he made, Musgrove would deposit in banks under various names, and Henry Thompson could never figure this out, since he'd never known Musgrove to return to these places, unless the man had someone else closing out these accounts. The last two were Carney Williams and John "Three-fingered Jack" Dunlop. Whenever the gang split up, these two left together, probably to go back to Walnut Ridge, down in Arkansas. These men were the survivors, as many of their kind had been gunned down or left to dangle at the end of a rope. Thompson felt good about the chilling fact all of them were weaned to killing.

His musings were interrupted by Black Jack. "Henry, tomorrow we head out of here for the Missouri Breaks. To a place called Cow Island Landing; you ever heard of it?"

"Forlorn as hell around there. All them breaks and Cow Creek and the Bearpaws to the north—even U.S. marshals shy away from there." He didn't ask but reckoned this was where they'd hook up with whoever was bankrolling them, and what's more, at the moment Long Henry didn't really give a hoot. He knew Black Jack would handle things right. His eyes stabbed out at Sixtoes Baker dipping his hand inside the blouse of the whore sharing a rickety chair, and Thompson had to grin. Yup, he mused grandly, with Sixtoes and the High Fives on the loose up here and raisin' all kinds of sweet hell, life won't be so boring. The whore who'd been with him had left his side. And deciding that a woman was what he wanted, he flicked out a summoning finger, and a whore he'd been exchanging glances with shot over to his table like she'd just been squeezed out of a tube of petroleum jelly. "Black Jack, I'm headin' up into the hayloft to fed this filly some rolled oats. Be back to chaw some more over some prime beefsteaks."

* * *

Until five months ago Shorty Huckabee had been working down at the shipping pens in Great Falls. He was the kind of person nobody took too seriously, as besides being runty he had a hard time framing the right words. The few bucks he'd earned he used to purchase a stagecoach ticket, the driver kicking him off in Loma, where Huckabee settled in real quickly. His first job was as the local garbageman's helper, the pair of them going around town picking up garbage and hauling it out to the city dump. Figuring the rats out there were as big as he was, he managed to talk town marshal Dan Clemens into taking him on.

It was a job that saw Shorty Huckabee cleaning out the jail and otherwise running errands for Clemens. Mostly as a joke, Clemens had sworn Huckabee in as a deputy town marshal, and then made his runty deputy patrol the streets at night while Dan Clemens hung out at the Blue Moon Saloon playing four-handed cutthroat pinochle with his cronies.

One thing you could say for Shorty Huckabee, the twenty-nine-year-old drifter hung in there every night along with watching over the city jail during the day. The fact Clemens wouldn't let him pack a gun for fear Huckabee would probably injure himself had for a time stung his pride. Yet it was on one of these lonely nightly sojourns along the alley passing in back of the local bank that Shorty Huckabee gained some notoriety and respect, as he'd come across a couple of drunks trying to break into the bank.

Unarmed, and about to say to hell with this and skedaddle, Huckabee soon noticed the two men could hardly stand much less use the crowbar they had to pry the back door open. When one of them suddenly sagged down and passed out, the terror of western lawmen saw his chance. Groping on the muddy ground for an empty whiskey bottle, he latched on to it to creep in on the would-be bank robbers. Later on it came to Huckabee that he could have blown a train whistle in the ears of the man crouching there as he tried rousing his would-be partner in crime. Instead, he swung the bottle, breaking it over the head of the man holding the crowbar, whose gun Shorty Huckabee then grabbed and fired warning shots into the air.

Out of this Huckabee received a lot of disbelieving looks from the locals and, as a reward from banker Cyrus Spurgeon, was treated to a hot beef sandwich over at the Red Dot Cafe, along with a free toothpick. This was the way things had stood for Shorty Huckabee until the day a stranger rode into Loma to rob the Stockman's Bank. Not only did the bank robber clean out the vault, but, it was suspected that he departed in the company of local bartender Buck Green.

And so it was that Shorty Huckabee, with the absence of the town marshal, found himself in charge of a posse trying to track down the bank robber. Much as the sparrows return to Capistrano, the dwindling members of the posse felt their best chance of catching the bank robber was down at Shonkin, and tonight under a full moon they were closing in on the settlement as attested to by Highwood Peak holding in the near distance.

Everyone would have quit long before had not banker Spurgeon put up a five-hundred-dollar reward. Even so, about half of the original twenty had peeled back for Loma, leaving mostly those who had accounts with the bank, or otherwise felt Cyrus Spurgeon would hold it against them if they didn't see this through.

The discussion of the bank robber's identity had consumed their talk along the way. One wag now said, "Maybe we should have brought that waitress along, you know, Loraine, so's she could identify certain parts of this gent's body."

"Keep comin' up with gems like that, Ernie, and we'll run you for mayor. So, Mister Huckabee, sir, yonder's Shonkin."

"Don't I know it," Huckabee responded in his high falsetto. Like everyone else—he knew it and so did they—now that the dreaded hangout of the high liners had been reached, he was scared to the point of dismounting and taking another leak before he accidentally stained himself.

"Half the night is shot," someone said plaintively.

Another member of the posse removed his hat and used his bandanna to wipe the sweat from his face. "So what," he said, "those sin-holes in there never close."

"You really think Buck Green is with this bank robber?"

"Whatta we know about Buck other than he drifted in not all that long ago."

"I say we send out a point rider to get the lay of it in there."

By common accord everyone turned their attention to Shorty Huckabee, who was squatting tiredly aboard his grain-fed gelding. He had on old, patched Levi's and a woolen shirt with the sleeves rolled up to his elbows to reveal his thin arms. A badge glittered on his chest, and right now he was tempted to discard the damned thing when Butch Yates, more or less the town bully, said, "You know, Shorty, Mr. Spurgeon put you in charge of this posse. So it's your duty to go in and scout them saloons out. Ain't that right?"

"Yeah, Butch, how do we know Buck Green or this bank robber ever showed up here. I doubt there's any truth to the rumor this gent is that gunfighter, Henry Thompson. Man with his rep sure wouldn't hold up a piss-ant bank or even come into a hole like Loma. What we'll do, Shorty, as you ride in, is pull in around Shonkin. Hell, all it is, is about a half-dozen buildings, and some whores." His cackling laughter chased up some smiles.

"Reckon," stammered Huckabee, "I can look Shonkin over. Yup"—he tried to frame a smile, but it didn't come off—"this Long Henry Thompson might notta robbed the bank after all."

"Well, get, then."

And Shorty Huckabee got, jabbing his spurs sharply into the flanks of the gelding, which, tired as it was, shot ahead a couple of steps before settling into the rhythm of a don't-give-a-hoot canter. That he was scared showed under moonlight in how Shorty gripped the reins and began checking to make sure his sixgun was still in its holster. At the moment he had this powerful urge to wheel up and pull out his carrot and let it stream, but then a door swung open in a saloon less than forty rods away to let out pale yellow light and an hombre reeling under the load of a full belly of rotgut. The man staggered around the corner of the building, and Huckabee muttered, "Lordy, it was just a drunk, hoss. Damn Dan Clemens anyhow for taking off. But, Shorty, you is now Marshal Huckabee . . . an' there's this big cash reward to whoever arrests this bank robber . . ."

Figuring discretion was the better part of valor, he swung over and reined up by a deserted building which formed part of the street passing in front of this and the other saloons. He was tempted to take his Winchester rifle, but left it in the saddle boot, and turned and hefted his gunbelt as his short legs took him angling toward the saloon he'd passed. The drunk reappeared and went back into the saloon without spotting Huckabee, who'd suddenly realized a Colt .45 could put a big hole in the badge he wore, and quickly he unpinned it and stuffed it into his shirt pocket.

"Undercover work," he said by way of a lame alibi. Swiveling his head about, he felt a little better when he sighted some of the posse ghosting out a ways from the buildings and finding places of concealment. Derision flared in his eyes. "Bunch of damned windbags—especially that Butch Yates. The only thing they've ever fired off is their big mouths."

When he came into the frame of light radiating out from the open door, Huckabee had second thoughts about this, but to his credit he went on, the spurs he'd put on for no useful reason other than they looked good on his scuffy boots chiming out his approach. Stepping up to clear the doorsill, he saw to his disappointment the small saloon was empty but for the drunk trying to pick up a whiskey bottle with both hands and a lonely bartender.

Bolstered by this, Shorty Huckabee walked on in and sidled up to the plank bar, the bartender making no effort to heave up from the high stool he was perched on. "Son, we don't serve those who ain't passed through puberty yet."

"Well, lookit here, Mr. Bartender, this silver dollar says otherwise."

"Another cattle baron," grunted the barkeep as he reached back for a whiskey bottle. "You want I should mix it with warm milk, or can you handle this panther piss."

"Any strangers been in here lately?"

"You, sonny. Shit, everyone comes here is a stranger."

"I'm lookin' for two men; one of them is named Buck Green . . . an' the other is a real tall gent."

"That a fact. They your Sunday School teachers, or what . . ."

"Well, have they been here," demanded Huckabee as he took the whiskey in the shot glass down clean and never so much as blinked an eye. He slammed the shot glass down, to mutter loudly, "Fill it up, bardog."

"That . . . that big ol' mean gunslick givin' . . . givin' you trouble, Ted . . ."

The barkeep glanced at the drunk, but refrained from saying anything. He refilled the shot glass, then muttered, "That'll be another silver dollar. Big tall man, you said?" He had a pimpled, unshaven face, and now a smile glittered in his hard eyes. This runt, he speculated, must be from Loma, as he knew all about that bank job, having overheard Long Henry Thompson state matter-of-factly just how easy it had been. "You the law or something . . ."

"Yup, Marshal Huckabee."

"Well, sir, a drifter came through, oh, last night it were, told me the bank over at Loma had been hit. As you can see, there ain't nobody in here but me and Rufus Smit . . . so I reckon you'd better try your luck at the other saloons . . . an' don't forget the silver dollar. Obliged, and you never told me if you was a U.S. marshal or not as you ain't got a badge peeled to your shirt."

Passing out the door, Huckabee stifled the urge to tell the smartass bartender where he could go, while back inside, the man was coming out from behind his bar. "Rufus, take over 'til I get back; and watch what you drink or I'll skin you alive."

"Where you goin', Ted—"

"To watch a sideshow that's about to take place," he threw over his shoulder while putting on his hat as he strode toward the back door.

The second saloon checked out by Shorty Huckabee was in the same deserted condition as the first; but from the sustained noise coming from the last building in town, the big, barnlike structure, he knew some high riders were in there, and uneasily he headed that way, passing as he did a corral holding several horses. Veering closer, he slid his eyes over some unfamiliar brands adorning the flanks of the horses. If he would have taken more time, he would have seen a couple of brands he knew, but in his present frame of mind it was all he could do to keep on going.

"By rights, dammit, we should'a all ridden in and arrested ev'ry son'bitch here. But no, Yates had to put in his two cents worth. So, here I am . . . and what's that?" His head popped sideways at the hellish snarl made by a tomcat spitting out its intention to another cat it was chasing, and at that, Marshal Huckabee let go to water his inner thighs, but managed to choke off the rest of it. "I'll . . . that damned cat . . ." He stood there, shaking and otherwise all nerved up. Right now the scourge of U.S. marshals had the strong wish to be back in Great Falls shoveling shit at the stockyards. But, calming down some, he knew to cut and run now would not only destroy any credibility he had, but give Butch Yates all the rope he needed to make him the laughingstock of Loma.

"Somethin' that potbellied slob would enjoy," he muttered, going on. An idea began forming in which the wisest course of action, in The Barn, according to the unimaginative sign nailed above the front door, was to go in quietly and take in the action. He could pass himself off as a cowhand passing through in search of work.

Moving on again, he was unaware of the bartender he'd confronted a few minutes ago stealing by in the deeper shadows behind the saloon. The barkeep, Ted Murdock, came in the back door and looked about rather anxiously for the big gent, Henry Thompson. As he wanted to pick up a few bucks by warning Thompson; then his eyes landed on the other one, Sixtoes Baker, and he slipped up to Baker's table and sat down without being invited.

"Where's Mr. Thompson?"

"Upstairs," Baker said surly. "Yeah, you're a barkeep. So whatta you want?"

"To warn you that a lawman just left my place and is headin' here, Mr. Baker. I doubt if he's alone, that he's part of a posse."

"You hear that, Black Jack."

"Yup, Sixtoes," the outlaw responded around a grin. And the grin held when in through the open doorway came Huckabee, Black Jack's questioning eyes flicking back to the bartender. "That . . . is Mr. John Law? Man, I'll bet he can't even see over the bar top to order a drink. At least he had enough smarts not to wear a badge. So, Sixtoes, what's it to be?"

Now Buck Baker recognized the would-be lawman as someone he knew from Loma. He knew the town would send out a posse, remembering now that the regular town marshal had taken off someplace for a few days, but to place Huckabee in charge of a posse was to him an act of the utmost desperation, until one recalled just how greedy banker Cyrus Spurgeon was.

"That runt ain't alone, I can tell you that, Black Jack."

"A posse, huh? If they're of the same cut of cloth as that runt, all we gotta do is light a firecracker and throw it out the door and they'll skedaddle."

"I'll go brace Marshal Huckabee." Sixtoes Baker shoved the whore's encircling arm away, and Ted the bartender slipped into the shadows.

"Take it slow, Sixtoes, as things are damned dull around

here. Let 'em eyeball us desperadoes a little longer before you make your move. S'matter of fact, Shirley, if that's your name, sidle up to Mr. Runt Lawman and—"

"But, gee, Black Jack, he's so small . . ."

"Then cuddle him in your lap." He laughed.

Where he stood by the bar, Shorty Huckabee took in Buck Green sitting with some woman, and Huckabee knew they'd struck pay dirt. On the verge of leaving, he was suddenly aware of the sweet scent of perfume. He found its source was a henna-haired woman. Brushing herself close to him, she whispered, "What's a hunk of man like you doin' in a place like this, sugah?"

"Ah . . . ah, ma'am, thank you kindly but I'm just leaving."

She leaned in closer and kissed Shorty Huckabee on the cheek, leaving the imprints of her lips behind, and he reddened as she said, "That's worth at least a shot of Old Crow, Mister Man."

"Yeah, what the hell, sure." He found himself being swung around to face the bar and the oversized bartender waiting to take his order, not picking up on the fact those who'd been standing at the bar had faded back to the tables or were leaving. He had exactly three silver dollars left and some smaller change. One drink with this lady wouldn't hurt, he figured, as he dug out his money. "What's your name?"

"Shirley LaRue . . . of the Nob Hill LaRues, sugah . . . and what about you?"

"Oh," he hesitated, "Orville Huckabee, but they call me—"

"Orville's just dandy. You wanna go upstairs and help me look through my family scrapbook, Orville honey?"

"Ain't got time, but here's mud in your eye, ma'am, ah, Shirley."

"You done stole my woman!"

"Me, I . . ." Huckabee dropped the shot glass as he pushed clear of the woman to see Buck Green coming toward the bar, and with his right hand hovering by his holstered sixgun.

"Clear your ass outta the way, Shirley, as this little pipsqueak is mine."

"Look, Buck, it's me, Shorty Huckabee. Don't you remember me swampin' out your bar a few times . . ."

"Cut the crap, Shorty. What's that tinny thing stickin' out of the top of your shirt pocket."

"Oh, shit," threw out Huckabee as he swung his eyes down to his pocket. "Look, Buck, it ain't me that come alone . . . got thirty more out there . . . got Shonkin damned surrounded. Now if you had anything"—he began backing toward the open doorway, careful to keep his hand away from his holstered gun—"to do with that bank robbery, why, Buck, just stay clear of this thing. Shirley, you want Shirley, she's yours."

"Why, you little shit ass," the woman shot out.

"It's me he wants!" The voice of Henry Thompson struck down loudly from where he stood on the upper landing, stark naked but for the Colt .45 he was holding. And everyone in the barroom froze where they were. Even Sixtoes Baker expected to get caught with a slug in the upcoming violence, for they all knew, everyone but Shorty Huckabee easing to frame himself in the open doorway, the explosive temper of Long Henry.

It was as Huckabee took a longer backward step and was about to whirl about and flee that Henry Thompson's gun belched out flame and a leaden slug that struck the little man in the right eye, the force of the bullet flinging him outside. He was dead before he hit the ground.

It was here that Black Jack Christian pulled out his gun and broke toward the front door, as he figured that at any moment the posse would come in with blazing guns. Pushing up against the door frame, he stood there seeking a target for his gun. But what he didn't expect to see was a bunch of riders pulling out frantically to the north on the main trail.

He dropped his gun to his side, busting a gut laughing, as he managed to say, "After Wyatt Earp here got gunned down, the rest of those heroes from Loma cut out like some wasps was after them."

Up on the landing, Henry Thompson grunted out gutturally, "Man can't even get fixed up proper around this here Shonkin." Then he stalked out of sight. Through his displeasure he wondered if he should reveal to Black Jack the details of another recent killing. "Nope, he'll find out soon enough about that, too—glad we're haulin' ass come sunup."

SIX

In between where the Judith and Musselshell rivers flowed into the Missouri the forbidding breaks pushed down into central Montana. These breaks were composed of deep gullies and scrub brush and smaller creeks creating an almost impenetrable maze covering hundreds of square miles. Cowmen would turn their stock loose to graze and hope they could find the bulk of their herds during fall roundup. The breaks were thick with mule deer and smaller game, and now in late spring a few flocks of Canada geese were still pushing up into Canada as this was part of a great flyway extending eastward into the Dakotas. Not only did it afford excellent cover and foliage for livestock, but it was an excellent place to hunt. Sometimes old bones of some long-dead outlaw or someone who'd just gotten lost in the breaks would be found, as well as the remains of cabins. No towns had ever been built up here, though there were some deserted settlements strung out along the Missouri River.

One of these places was Cow Island Landing, which cut into the river from the north, and was a good place to push cattle across. North of this was a pretentious knob of rock called the Little Rocky Mountains, which were really high hills, and just to the west lay the Bearpaws and in between these heights meandered Cow Creek. Farther to the west, say about forty miles in a fairly straight line from the breaks, lay Judith Landing, named for the river of the same name. And then west a couple of dozen miles Slaughter River and Hole-in-the-Wall landings.

The trouble was that the boats which had brought commerce

up the Missouri no longer were needed. So the buildings at these landings had been left to rot away. One prominent landmark was the old Power-Norris freight warehouse, a huge stone building professionally mortared, and though deserted, it was weathering well. Sometimes in inclement weather cowpokes out rounding up strays would come in here to dry out and maybe camp for a day or two. West of the ferry landing and on the south shore, buried beneath a corner of the building, was the body of a boy of around seven, killed when hit in the head by a singletree on one of the freight wagons loading at the docks. They say the ghost of little Boyd Norris sometimes prowled about on summery nights when heat lightning stung at the sky—with one overnighter swearing he'd actually talked to the boy. Despite this, cowhands still came in on those rare times when their job brought them to the landing.

Not all that far away was located the site of Fort Clagett, a little-known army post which the hostile Sioux attacked repeatedly. Rotting away now, it was surrounded by a lot of debris the cavalrymen left when they pulled out—whiskey bottles, buttons from cavalry coats, a myriad of square, handmade nails and .70 and .80 caliber bullets, and other rusty debris spilled around the blacksmith shops.

This was the place the High Fives and the two new members of the gang, Henry Thompson and Sixtoes Baker, pulled into after they'd left Shonkin two days ago. Not being all that anxious to spend the night in the ruins of the fort, even though the sun had sank away about an hour ago, a word from Black Jack Christian kept all of them saddlebound where they'd pulled up to take a breather. The river water was high this time of year, and it pushed in against the rotting pier down by the landing.

Brushing at the mosquitos swarming around him, Thompson said distastefully, "I've seen the Missouri before; but not from such a lonely spot. How far to where your man from Havre'll meet us?"

"West of here a couple of miles, Henry. According to this map he sent me."

"All I can say is, Black Jack, he's a cautious son'gun. Just so he has our money," he said threateningly. "I'm about as hungry as a quilled dog; so this silent partner of yours better have supper waitin' when we pull in."

"Sure as dogs suck eggs, Henry, we'll all chow down."

Three-Fingered Jack Dunlop muttered, "Our hosses can rest when we get there, so dammit, let's go." He was a surly-faced Texan gone bad when going on thirteen years old he bushwhacked a gold miner coming in from some forlorn place. Ever since, the killings and crimes had piled up until today he was about the most wanted man in this bunch of high riders. He always lagged behind when they rode someplace, Bob Hays jesting about this being caused by all the lead Dunlop carried in his body from numerous bullet wounds. None of his companions in crime knew he was one of nine children sired by a Pentecostal sky pilot.

Tired, and owlish, and out of hard liquor, it wasn't long before the High Fives pushed through some more scrub trees and brush, having to ride here because of a sheer bluff dropping down to the riverbank. George Musgrove threw out some blue-heater cuss words when a thorny branch released by Will Christian riding in front of him whipped back to lash him across the face. Now, out front, Black Jack and Henry Thompson felt a little better when they saw the glow of a camp fire lighting up the side wall of the old Power-Norris freight warehouse building, and back in the shadows some packhorses. But cautiously the outlaws held up as Black Jack called out, "Hello the fire . . . you mind if some thirsty cowpunchers ride on in . . ."

"Yup, as good company is hard to come by in these parts."

Closer, the outlaws could make out at least four men by the camp fire, three of them wearing rough clothing, the fourth attired in clothes more suited to cowtown living. Now they realized there were actually two camp fires, the other one out back of the building where another man was tending to some big black-bottomed kettles around which flames were eating.

As the outlaws swung in closer and climbed out of their

saddles, Ralph Glendenning, one of the men by the camp fire, stepped over and thrust out his hand to Black Jack. "Mr. Christian, it's a pleasure meeting you at last. We've been camped here for the last three days. Not all that bad as the fishing's good, and it was enjoyable getting away from Havre."

"You sure picked a lonely spot for this meeting."

"The fewer know about this the better."

"My sentiments, Mr. Glendenning. Your contact down in Greeley filled me in on some of what we'll be doing. Been a while getting up here; and I hope we'll pull out before winter as I detest a cold spell." Black Jack's eyes swept over the other men who'd been waiting. "Your partners?"

"Actually, Black Jack, these are the men you'll turn the cattle you rustle over to . . . which I'll explain after we eat, as I figure you boys are plumb tuckered out."

"They're French-Canadian—"

"Canucks," Glendenning verified as he walked with Black Jack along the side wall toward the spot where everyone else was already lining up to eat. "They want all the beef we can get our hands on."

"Meaning we'll be hazing any stock we rustle over the border."

"Where these Canucks will be waiting to pay us cash on the barrel head and then take the cattle off our hands."

"Reckon it beats all the hassle of selling this stock here in Montana. I hear the stock association hereabouts is hell on wheels when it comes to checkin' ownership of cattle on the hoof. You know, Mr. Glendenning, I got you pegged as a gent livin' a pretty good life. Just why are you gettin' involved in this kind of operation—or maybe this is none of my business."

This was a question that of late even Ralph Glendenning found hard to answer. Part of the answer lay back in St. Louis. There he'd been a prominent trial lawyer, and his clients had included a few criminal figures. He had enjoyed the kind of notoriety he'd gained in defending these men in court. Until that fateful day came when he'd witnessed one of his clients kill in cold blood a St. Louis assistant district attorney. Glendenning knew that if he told the truth in court he'd be found at the bottom of the Mississippi River. Soon afterward he simply pulled out, going to Santa Fe, only to be tracked down there by an investigator holding a warrant for his arrest. Forewarned by a lawman he'd befriended, Ralph Glendenning decided this time to head up into the northern reaches of Montana.

And Havre, he had found, was about as far as a man could get before striking into the barren plains of Canada. At first it was tough going, as a man had to be accepted by local politicians even up in this large cattle town. He did make enough to purchase a modest house; the rest of what he took in he spent on gambling or on taking a few out-of-town trips. Perhaps it had always been in him, this evil seed, which caused him to realize in a way he was no different than those criminals he had defended down in St. Louis. If he could make a shady buck or two, what the hell, wasn't this what made the world go around.

Opportunity had reared its beckoning head for Ralph Glendenning on a business trip up to Medicine Hat, in Alberta. Here in this old-time cowtown east of the Canadian Rockies cattle buyers would come in hoping to sell cattle to beef-starved cities like Edmonton and Winnipeg. Through here also passed rolling stock of the Canadian Pacific line. It was at the Golden Spur Gambling Emporium that he had first encountered Pierre LaFleur, of French-Canadian descent, and possessed of high cheekbones in a hawkish face.

"Seems I saw you out at the sale barn, Mr. LaFleur . . ."

"Just seeking out old friends. So you're managing the N Bar N; I knew Charlie Price real well. So now the N Bar is owned by some absentee owners—"

"About all they're interested in is how much profit they can make."

"And don't know beans about ranching. I know the kind. How many head of beef do you plan to sell, Mr. Glendenning?"

"Depends," he said evasively, where they stood by the crowded bar and gazed out at the gambling action.

"You a gambler . . ."

"If you call losing at cards gambling, guess I am. Why?"

The answer to this came later that night in the form of a proposition from Pierre LaFleur. They were enjoying a late supper at a different casino, and in the background honky-tonk music sounded amidst the action at the tables. "So, Ralph, the people we sell livestock to will overlook such things as brands and bills of sale. You just drive up a herd; my men'll take over from there."

"Pushing them on to this slaughter house over in Saskatchewan."

"This will take some thought—to organize things, a man'll have to have some seed money."

"I'm willing, monsieur, to invest in this once you determine how much you'll need." Picking up the wine bottle, he refilled their glasses. "You mentioned getting the right men to, shall we say, steal the cattle."

"That," agreed Glendenning, "and a way to get around those stock detectives down there. You can't buy them off like you can other lawmen. Do you have any suggestions, Pierre?"

"There is always a way," he said softly, to add ominously, "there is also the silence of the grave."

This was the moment of truth, Ralph Glendenning realized. That Pierre LaFleur hadn't spoken idly lay naked in the man's eyes. And what did he have to look forward to back in Havre, but his seedy law practice and that one day a lawman would show up and he'd be dragged back to St. Louis. He said, "Yes, this has to be done by professionals."

"And I know just the men. I made their acquaintance a few years back when I spent the winter down in New Mexico. Their leader is Black Jack Christian; perhaps you've heard of him?"

Frowning, Glendenning finally said, "Yes, he's leader of the High Fives—but do you think, Pierre, they'll come this far north . . ."

The answer came after Pierre LaFleur had sent a letter to a certain post office box down in Taos, New Mexico. Black Jack was certainly interested in striking into territory where he hadn't committed any crimes before. And now as Ralph Glendenning walked alongside Black Jack to come around the warehouse, he said, "I've already had something done that'll keep the law away from our rustling operation."

Black Jack said, "Meanin' you're payin' some local lawmen under the table—"

"Better than that, in that my recommendation helped a certain cowhand become the new stock inspector for this area. I'll tell you more about it after we've chowed down. You remember Pierre LaFleur . . ."

The French-Canadian approached the two men.

"Yup, and that letter you sent, LaFleur"—they shook hands—"came when we needed another place to operate in."

"The big thing in our favor," said LaFleur, "is there's an open border and you seldom run across a Mountie. Once you turn the cattle over to me and my Canucks, we hand over your money. I have brought along some maps to show you, Black Jack. I'm excited about having you join us."

"There's seven of us to start with," Black Jack told both of them. "We might need more help, and if so, Henry Thompson will tend to that."

"I'll tell you now, Black Jack," said Glendenning, "a few small gangs have already done some rustling. There's the Hayward bunch . . . paid them to do a little chore for me." He saw no need to tell his new partners these outlaws had killed the previous stock inspector. And like he had promised, once they'd chowed down, the three of them congregated inside the warehouse while their men held outside by camp fires set back in the trees to avoid detection. An old work table in one of the rooms used as an office had been cleared of debris, and by lamplight they studied LaFleur's map.

As Glendenning said, "The trick is to appease these ranchers. By having some of these rustlers arrested. Like the Hayward gang."

"How you fixin' to do this?"

"Simply by telling this stock inspector where to look for them."

Still filled with skepticism, Black Jack shot back, "Won't he suspect something you comin' up with the location of these rustlers—"

"Of course he will. But Nick Dunn won't have any choice in the matter. Let's leave it at that." Ralph Glendenning jabbed a finger at an area south of the Sun River. "Summer range for the Fairweather ranch is this general area. Jesse Fairweather and his men are part of the Shelby roundup. Though his cattle have already been rounded up and worked, the roundup has moved away down here to the southeast—probably in the middle of branding on the Kettledrum ranch. Back here now, Fairweather's cattle have been turned loose to graze, but they still should be fairly close together."

"Sounds good," said Black Jack. "At the most there won't be over three or four 'pokes tending to these cattle. An' if they give us any trouble, the way it goes . . ."

Pierre LaFleur said, "Remember, east of this you'll find that the Box Elder roundup is still going on. The first herd or two we'll drive them straight north. Past Willow Creek you'll run into more rugged country just south of the border. There's a butte here to guide you to where we'll take over."

"These roundups goin' on makes rustlin' a heap easier."

"It'll be harder once the ranchers are back on their respective ranches. At which time I turn Nick Dunn loose to hunt down these rustlers." Glendenning returned their smiles, feeling better now that everything was being laid out. About Christian there was this aura of self-confidence. While eating, Henry Thompson's name had been brought up in that he knew the country, all the way from the Missouri Breaks clear to the Rockies. So these night forays would have a high chance of being successful.

"Later on, Black Jack, I'd suggest you drive the cattle due east into the breaks. As up on the Missouri there are some good crossings."

"And we're paying so much per head," said LaFleur, "that if you have to run them and they come in a little gaunted, they can still be ground into sausage. In the morning we will take you and the supplies to some deserted buildings about five miles away. But here, this money will seal our deal."

"Not bad for starters," said Black Jack as he stabbed a glance at the greenbacks in the manila envelope. "West of here, as Long Henry told me, is Blackfoot country hooking into the Rockies. We could run some cattle north along them mountains, too."

"The Red Miller gang is holed up someplace in those parts," said Glendenning. "I'll make sure the word goes out they are the actual rustlers, and then Nick Dunn moves in to bring them to justice."

"One thing I gotta mention," said Black Jack, "is that this Nick Dunn you keep bringing up had a run-in with Henry Thompson. Out when they both worked for the N Bar ranch."

"I'll speak to Dunn about this when we get together."

"Just what is it about this Dunn?"

"Like I said to Pierre, you boys leave Nick Dunn to me. From here on in I'll be out of the picture. It wouldn't do for the ranchers or people in Havre to find out we're business partners. Pierre or one of his men will be my liaison to you, Black Jack. That's about it, other than let's make this a summer these Montana ranchers will never forget." Glendenning pulled out a flask and unscrewed the cap, after which he passed the flask to Black Jack.

"Reckon I can drink to that, Mr. Glendenning. With you in cahoots with the law and with the help of Pierre, here, the odds are long in our favor."

SEVEN

At no time in his life had Starky True, aka Nick Dunn, ever expected to be part of the lawmen's outlaw-fetching fraternity. When the bossman out at the N Bar, Tom Wilson, had singled him out with news the stockman's association wanted him to be one of their stock inspectors, it had taken a lot of effort for Nick Dunn to keep the disbelief from bubbling out into words, or to keep a straight face. He'd accepted the offer only after learning that the new job would keep him out on the range instead of in cowtowns where he stood the chance of being recognized. And besides, another thing easing Nick's fears was that wanted posters would be sent to his new post office box over in Box Elder. Those bearing his likeness he could destroy.

He would soon take up residence in a house the local banker owned, which lay buried amid elm and cedar trees on a vague back street. Not only was he to get a hefty salary, but a horse and money for supplies and new guns, too. Plus, every rancher belonging to the association was duty-bound to render the new stock inspector assistance. One of the first chores undertaken by Nick was to introduce himself to town marshal Parker Dillingham, and then have a Box Elder gunsmith rework his guns.

His first few days in town Nick spent at the Carbine Hotel, which was being managed now by a woman named Vivian McCauley. One day Nick had come into the hotel dining room to be waved over by Marshal Dillingham, who was seated at a table with Vivian, the marshal saying, "Vivian, I want you to meet our new brand inspector. Nick Dunn worked out at the N Bar, too.

Right away he'd liked the way sunlight touched upon Vivian McCauley's auburn hair and the fact she was rather good-looking. After the marshal had left, he stayed at the table with her simply because she was easy to talk to, but it wasn't until a couple of days later that he got up enough courage to ask her out for Sunday dinner. Another thing he liked about Vivian was that she hadn't questioned where he had come from.

And so for Nick Dunn his first Saturday night in Box Elder passed quietly, where he got himself hooked up in a poker game at a saloon. Along with the badge, he'd been given a list of names of suspected rustlers and general locations of where to find these hombres. He should have cut out in the middle of the week, and would have, but tomorrow Havre lawyer Ralph Glendenning would be coming in to palaver with him. It was chiefly because of Glendenning's recommendation that he'd gotten this job.

Now, as he went on foot toward Main Street, and slicked out in some new duds, he forgot about Glendenning showing up, for he was on his way to meet Vivian McCauley at the Carbine Hotel. He'd picked up on the fact she was more or less considered Tom Wilson's girl, not from Vivian but from bar talk. As for Nick, it had been years, by his mental tally, since he'd been around a respectable woman. Over these years he'd picked up a rough edge to his words, and for sure he'd have to watch so that no damns or other swear words slipped out unbidden.

If only those lawmen down in Wyoming could see me now. A smile etched across his face when he saw through a lobby window Vivian McCauley rising from a chair, and quickly he entered.

"Good morning, Mr. Dunn." Her smile included the desk clerk. She wore a floor-length dress and carried a parasol. Other than the three of them the lobby was empty, though a few people were in the dining room. And it was a sunlit day, the sky a deep blue and cut here and there with fluffy white clouds. Vivian inhaled deeply of the still air as they passed down the street. "Sometimes I get the notion to go back to Boston, Nick, and once I did. I managed to last a month. Once you set eyes upon the mountains, where else can one live."

"My sentiments, Vivian. You know, first time I've been saddled with pinnin' on a badge. Takes gettin' plumb used to."

"By now spring branding is winding down; how did Tom like being bossman for the Box Elder bunch?"

"A fine man, that Tom Wilson. I hear, Vivian, you and him are . . . friends . . ."

"Kind of, Mr. Dunn," she said pensively. "I have other men friends, as you call them." She returned the wave of some acquaintances now entering the Cedar Grove Cafe, which was housed in a big, rambling frame building upon which cedar trees threw plenty of shade. Strewn about amongst the trees were picnic tables and behind the building was a barbecue pit. A squirrel cut through a patch of grass and leaped up a tree trunk, and a few sparrows flitted overhead as he held the door to the cafe open for Vivian.

The room they entered was composed of booths and a long counter and a few tables; but Nick Dunn responded to the beckoning finger of a waitress, and in the large dining room he led Vivian to a window table. Removing his hat, he dropped it on an empty chair and began to relax more in the sheer enjoyment of talking to Vivian, who, he'd learned, had attended college, though she had never revealed her reasons for being way out here.

"Parker told me there's been some rustling."

"Marshal Dillingham ought to know," he said. "Some men just don't like to work if they can steal, I reckon."

At last for Tom Wilson the spring roundup had concluded and he could go back to check out things at the N Bar. For his fellow ranchers, there'd been some calf loss, as was to be expected. Most of those participating in the Box Elder roundup were of the opinion rustlers hadn't hit all that heavily, and to a man they were behind Nick Dunn's taking on the job of stock inspector.

After going back to the N Bar, Tom Wilson had seen that his men were given new tasks to perform before he and a couple of cowpokes took a supply wagon along to Box Elder. Clemet Hall was handling the team hitched to the big wagon while a little ways ahead rode Tom and Wyman Pruitt, who was as usual sitting his saddle with his left arm angled out. Pruitt had been jawing away, as usual, about nothing in general but that he liked to keep it rolling. Maybe, as Tom had mused back when breaking camp, it was that Wyman knew once he got back to Box Elder there might not be another spring roundup for him, and he just hated letting go. Though Tom didn't mind, since in between rambling on, his saddle companion would crack out a good joke.

"You know, when it's my time, I want to go quick like Jesse Snavely. No sawbones hangin' over me or wet nurse. That Henry Thompson, I wonder if they caught that sidewinder yet . . ."

"Probably not, Wyman," said Tom as now, upon getting his first glimpse of Box Elder and Big Sandy Creek, he was anxious to find out how Vivian McCauley had been faring. By rights, and this had been on his mind all during spring roundup, they should get hitched. Back in February he'd almost popped the question, but hadn't, for a number of reasons. The truth was, he admitted inwardly, maybe he was too old to change his ways. Besides, Vivian had others calling on her.

The road they had been on wasn't all that good, and they were thankful to rein their horses onto the main stagecoach road passing northerly; and Tom expected that Clemet Hall appreciated this even more, for glancing back, he grinned at the waddy rising a little from the hard wooden seat and rubbing his backside. He let the wagon catch up.

"Ain't bein' a 'poke a lot of fun, Clemet."

Shaking his head around a rueful smile, he said, "Just about the grandest job in this whole world, Mr. Tom. Now that you've been so considerate as to pay me, the first drink's on me when we hit town."

Proceeding for a couple more miles, they only realized it was Sunday when they sighted all the activity around the First Episcopal Church. They went on by, trail dusty and kind of anxious to find out the current news once they were in some saloon. Now the town folded around them, and soon Tom swung down before a livery stable. He would wait and leave tomorrow, since the mercantile stores were closed today, though he could have one of the merchants open up for them, especially since it was a two-day trip back to the N Bar. Anyway, he wasn't all that anxious to get back to picking up his bossing chores. Then there was Vivian to think about, too.

Inside the livery stable, they went about the chore of removing the saddles while Clemet released the harnesses from his pair of horses. The hostler was probably at home and wouldn't be in until tomorrow, so they spread clean straw in the stalls and pitched down hay for their horses. The last to come out was Tom Wilson, who gazed questioningly at Wyman Pruitt looking upstreet with an intense stare. Wyman turned now and said to Tom, "Wasn't sure, but I believe it was that lawyer fellow from Havre just pulling into town, same's us. Brought his hoss into Bellow's livery stable.

"Glendenning, you mean?"

"Yeah, and why they let him manage the N Bar has eluded my intelligence so far, Tom."

More to himself, Tom said, "Got no claim on his time; but he could'a told me he'd be comin' to Box Elder." And what rankled him even more was that Ralph Glendenning should have been out there during spring roundup, to at least make a pretense of watching out for the interests of the N Bar. "Anyway, Wyman, you did a good job as tallyman. Most like me can't count over ten."

"I seen you sweatin' over them ledger books out there, Mr.

Wilson. Which by rights should be that lawyer's job. What say we try Bertie's place, as I want'a pay off my bar tab."

Just as they approached the saloon, Tom Wilson took a final glance farther upstreet to catch a glimpse of Vivian McCauley coming out of the Cedar Grove Cafe. He hesitated, with the thought of going on to see her. Now Nick Dunn pushed through the screen door, and Tom was surprised to see the man fall in alongside Vivian. Instead of continuing along the street, they cut back to find a shaded picnic table, and masking his disappointment, Tom swung about and went into the saloon. If Tom Wilson would have remained in the street a few moments longer, he would have seen Ralph Glendenning emerge from a livery stable and cut across the street toward the cafe.

It was only by happenstance that Glendenning had spotted from within the stable Nick Dunn and the woman. He'd pulled out of the outlaw camp at sunup and was glad to get out of those breaks. And while fording the Missouri there'd been a scare as his horse had almost gone down. But here he was in Box Elder, pushing his hunger aside as he crossed the sidewalk and threw Dunn a casual wave.

"Been a spell, Nick."

"Sure has, Mr. Glendenning. This is Vivian McCauley."

"Ma'am." He touched the brim of his Stetson. "Sorry to barge in like this, but I detoured this way to discuss some things with Nick. After that I'm anxious to get back to Havre. Tell you what, Nick, I'll be in the cafe; if we could have a few moments alone, and then I'll be on my way." He left them back by the picnic table, smiling inwardly at the guarded look that had briefly touched Dunn's eyes. Entering the cafe, he was soon led to a table and was savoring a cup jaded with cream and a couple of sugar cubes.

It wasn't all that much longer before into the cafe came Nick Dunn, to plop down at Glendenning's table. Again the men shook hands, with Dunn being asked how he liked his new job. "Really can't tell yet," said Nick Dunn as a waitress paused with the pot she was holding to pour coffee into his cup. "One thing I do know, Ralph, I've got a lot of territory to cover—from east of here some clear over to the Rockies. You really went to bat for me on this, and I appreciate it."

The lawyer smiled and said, "You can handle it."

"Look," Nick said softly, "I reckon it's about time you laid this out for me. As to your particular interest in helpin' me out?"

"Things are about to take place, Nick, that can make both of us a lot of money. This involves making you a hero of sorts. And how am I going to do that? Simply by giving you detailed information on just where you can find certain rustlers. How does that sound?"

"You know, don't you . . ."

For a moment Glendenning didn't say anything. He glanced about the crowded dining room to make sure they weren't being overheard, and now he leaned in a little to say quietly, "That you're Starky True. Yes, I picked up on that about a week after you rode into Havre. I simply let this go, Mr. Dunn. And yes, part of my getting you a job out at the N Bar was to draw you into what's coming up."

"And that is?"

"I can't tell you all of it, Nick. Just that along with your regular salary my associates and I are putting aside some extra money which'll be yours if you keep on as stock inspector."

"Otherwise you'll tell some lawman I'm up here. I could draw down on you right now . . . and simply ride out of here . . ."

"And miss coming into some really big money? All I want is that you hang on until fall."

"You spoke of some rustlers. Could be that if you know where to find these high riders, Mr. Glendenning, you've been doing some kind of business with them."

"Let's just say that sometimes these men need a lawyer. Tell me, Nick, you ever heard of the High Fives, or of Black Jack Christian . . ."

"Just bar talk that they're outlaws out of the Nations."

"They're up here now, at my behest."

"And about to do some rustling, I suspect. What you just told me could see you arrested, too, Ralph."

"It could. It seems we have a standoff, Nick. You help me and I help you. Afterward, come fall, both of us'll have enough dinero to last a long time. So, it's your raise, Mr. Dunn—"

Nick refrained from speaking as a waitress set a plate of food before the lawyer. It pleased him, though he wouldn't tell Glendenning this, that others would be involved in this rustling scheme. That all he had to do was keep on packing this stock inspector's badge. He knew that the man across the table wasn't all that well-liked out at the N Bar. And while he'd been hanging around Havre, it appeared that Ralph Glendenning was just more or less tolerated, as were most Johnny-come-latelies in that close-knit town.

"I expect you've got your reasons for hooking up with these outlaws, and personally I don't give a whit why. I reckon I'll ante into your game, Ralph. You mentioned money . . ."

"I did, Nick, you'll get a percentage of our overall take. A man named Pierre LaFleur will pass through here during the summer and give you the money." He went on to specify to Nick Dunn just where the first raids against the herds of local ranchers would take place, that for convenience sake Nick should be elsewhere. "Go after the Haywards first. They've got a hideout due west someplace along Pondera Coulee. Four in this bunch, so you might need some help."

"No worry about that. As this breed'll be stretchin' hemp when some rancher gets his hands on 'em. Does anybody else back in Havre know who I am?"

"Just me, Nick."

"Was you, I'd keep it that way," he said ominously.

EIGHT

Back in the early '60's the Blackfeet had killed two white men trying to trap beaver along Coffee Creek. Time had passed, and the Indians had been driven farther west, so that now the creek and a big hunk of land between the Judith and Little Belt ranges was cattle country. The passage of the seasons was relatively unmarked by any exciting events, though a man did kill his wife down at Benchland.

For Rudy Steinbach it was just another peaceful summery night that he was enjoying astride his bronc while exchanging small talk with Eldon Chase, a man, at twenty-three, two years his senior. The pair of them, and three other Circle W hands, were keeping watch over what had been a larger herd of around four hundred head scattering out to graze. They were glad spring branding was over and they were back on the home ranch. To the west the creek was a natural barrier against too much drift by the cattle. Fence lines restricted the movement on the other three sides, but even so, fence posts went down and wire broke and a cowpoke spent a lot of time riding the fence line making repairs.

Steinbach's father ranched clear over by Wibaux, a small hardscrabble spread on which he raised nine children, the reason Rudy Steinbach took off about a year ago in look of work. He was a likeable young man with big cow eyes that had a lot of world to see yet. He took a lot of ribbing, especially from Eldon Chase, one of the few laying claim to being born in Montana. In their early twenties, the pair of them didn't have a care in the world, and once they hit the bunk in the bunkhouse or out here their bedrolls, they'd fall—much to the consternation of the older hands—into a dreamless sleep. Chase, an old hand at shaping tailor-mades, had gotten his saddle mate into this finger-staining habit, the smoke from their hand-rolleds hanging kind of wispy around them as the night was deadly still.

"If your pa does cash in his chips, Rudy, you ain't got much chance of takin' over the ranch."

"Got some younger brothers an' not all that much acreage. Why?"

"Me and you, Rudy, could go in as partners. Land's cheap over by the Rockies."

"You're forgettin', Eldon, about them Blackfeet. Even cheap as land is, we ain't got all that much cash anyway." He hazed his horse slowly along the fringe of grazing cattle, as not all that far away came the low-pitched whistle raised in song of another cowpoke. Contentment over his lot shone on Rudy Steinbach's face. Right now he wished this night would go on forever, the strong scent of the Mex tobacco in his hand-rolled filling his nostrils, along with the feel of a good horse under him. "Look at that quarter moon. I hear strange things happen when there's a full moon . . ."

"Seen some things," admitted Eldon Chase. He added pensively, "I wonder if they ever caught this gunslick who killed that N Bar cook."

"Might have, as everyone I know has been on the lookout for Long Henry Thompson. I hear he just up and shot that cook for no good reason a'tall."

"Hey, you two," came a twangy voice from behind them. "Keep on'a ridin' thataway and you'll tumble over yonder creek bank."

Now they realized the rising slope of land they were on had hidden the trees lining Coffee Creek, and somewhat sheepishly they reined their broncs around and went back toward Vince Lagon's vague and shadowy form slouched in his saddle.

Lagon was a grizzled, rough and tumble kind of waddy, with beard stubble crusting a moon face. Like them, he wore a holstered sixgun. But unlike these younger hands, Lagon was filled with a worry he couldn't shake.

He said roughly, "Tomorrow the cattle'll be spread out far enough so's we can leave them be and get busy on them fence lines. It must be goin' on ten at least. I sent Bucky and Ted down the creek more to build a camp fire. The cattle are drifting nice, so no sense watchin' them anymore tonight. You boys did bring along some extra grub in your saddlebags, I expect."

"You bet, Vince, I packed what I could."

"Seen young sprouts like you forget and go plumb hungry for a spell," he snapped out. He spurred his horse ahead at a walk, as he didn't want to take the chance of it stumbling into any gopher holes, which were common along western creeks.

Down in Texas and western Oklahoma the High Fives had turned their killing talents more to stagecoach or bank holdups than the more mundane chore of rustling cattle or horses. But that didn't mean they were any less skillful at hitting a herd of cattle and making a clean getaway. Along with being artful at blotting a brand and other outlaw tricks.

One thing would be different up here, and this the order just being issued by Black Jack Christian to the effect they'd leave no witnesses behind to identify them. This was one reason the High Fives had taken considerable pains in staying to rugged country in order to reach the Circle W Ranch, and had lain low during the day while taking in the five waddies hazing the large herd they planned to rustle northward along Coffee Creek.

Presently they were west of the creek, huddled under trees at a cold camp, and kind of anxious to get at it. But patiently Black Jack kept his men hunkered close to the trees and brush, until just a little while ago when Three-Fingered Jack Dunlop had ghosted back to say he'd spotted a camp fire.

"Two of them are by the camp fire, Black Jack. I expect the other three will be comin' in shortly expectin' some hot chow."

"Good, you know how we planned it."

"I got no argument with hangin' back," said Henry Thompson, "to let Sixtoes an' Jess and George operate on that pair of dumb-as-ox 'pokes."

"Yeah," muttered Sixtoes Baker, as if to pacify the big man. Though he was nervous as he mounted up along with the others, he knew the plan was as slick as they came. Fording the narrow creek, he broke away with two others to the north in the direction of the camp fire still a good mile away, leaving behind the rest of the High Fives holding close to the treeline.

With Sixtoes were George Musgrove and Jess Williams, and Sixtoes felt good that they had accepted him as an equal. They rode three abreast and loping their horses, and then Musgrove said quietly, "We just lope on in as they'll think it's the other three hands. You ever use a knife before?"

Sixtoes Baker muttered that he hadn't, momentarily wishing he were back holding with the main bunch. Then just like that they were coming over a ridgeline in the settled darkness of night and bobbing toward a big camp fire and the two men tending to the frying pans emitting the faint scent of bacon. One of the horses tied to a willow tree whickered a welcome. The outlaws had entered the halo of light cast out by the camp fire before one of the men there realized something was amiss, only it was too late.

"Don't!" Jess Williams snapped sharply. "Or I'll blow a hole in your brisket! The pair of you get on your bellies—do it now, dammit, or you're dead." He stared down coldly at the two cowhands dropping to the ground and over at Musgrove who was reaching for his hunting knife. Swinging a leg over the back of his saddle, Williams said to Sixtoes, "Cover 'em."

Side by side the outlaws crouched in on the two men stretched out on their bellies. They were both right-handed and held their knives in that hand, straddling their prey now, slapping the hats aside and then grabbing fistfuls of hair. Using their knees as weights to hold the men down, they wrenched the heads of the hapless waddies up and brought their razor-sharp knives down toward their throats in a quick cutting motion like butchers about to slaughter hogs. Blood splayed out as the men died, and just as quickly the bodies were dragged into underbrush. Coming back, Musgrove and Jess Williams picked up tin cups and filled them with hot coffee. They went over and hunkered down where one of the cowpokes had dropped his saddle and bedroll, and Sixtoes led their horses out of sight down by the creek.

For Buck "Sixtoes" Baker it had been a scary learning process, that the High Fives were simply cold-blooded killers of the highest order. He'd been scared shitless when he'd seen those knives used that way, and was still shaking as he tied up their horses. Unsheathing his Winchester, he came back to squat down near a fallen tree, where somehow his shaking hands worked the lever to eject a shell into the breech.

Sweat stung into one eye, and he cursed out, "That's all I need." His responsibility was to cover Musgrove and Williams, and he figured if he missed, they'd use those pigstickers on him. "Well, you was stupid enough to pard up with Long Henry. So settle down." The sound of a shod hoof striking a rock told him the other cowhands were coming in.

Over where they held by the campsite, the outlaws had their handguns out and concealed by their clothing. They were far enough away from the fire to be vague shadows to the men riding in. The first to emerge from the deeper shadows of night was Vince Lagon, who was just grateful that the day's riding was over and hot chow was in the offing. He bypassed the camp fire, casting an idle glance at the outlaws standing there and swung down where the other horses were tied up. Steinbach and Chase rode up now to do the same.

"Hey," Eldon Chase threw out as he began uncinching his saddle, "I just hope you ain't burnin' them beefsteaks." His back was to the outlaws slinking around the edges of the camp fire.

"Okay, hombres, elevate your arms!" snarled George Musgrove. He saw the uncertainty on the face of the older one, Lagon, and he added viciously, "Go for it then . . ." He fired his gun without allowing Lagon to jerk his sixgun out of its holster, and Lagon folded down in pain.

Just as quickly Jess Williams had responded by taking out Eldon Chase with a bullet through the chest, and another, and another, smiling mirthlessly and otherwise enjoying himself.

Only Rudy Steinbach remained alive, with his arms held rigidly over his head and stumbling back into his horse beginning to shy away from the sounds of violence and sudden death. A rifle sounded; the slug from it slapped into the side of the horse. Cursing, George Musgrove let his sixgun buck, and cowhand Steinbach screamed in pain and fear as he gaped in disbelief at the bullet hole in the middle of his chest. Then the rifle roared again, and Steinbach was slapped backward some by still another bullet striking into his midriff. He dropped dead to the ground.

"Okay," Musgrove called out to Sixtoes Baker. "They're dead. So mount up and fetch the others." He didn't bother with pawing through the pockets of the dead men as Williams was doing at the moment, the hunger in him driving him over to the camp fire, where he simply found a tin plate and plopped a beefsteak onto it and a mess of beans and went over to prop his back against a tree.

It wasn't long before the others rode in. After a brief discussion, it was decided to avail themselves of this campsite. Chiefly because the Circle W hands had been packing extra food, and Black Jack realized they weren't expected back for at least a week. Another determining factor was that the home buildings were at least eleven miles due south.

Black Jack let the men who'd done the actual killings finish eating supper before he told them to haul the bodies down under the prow of a creek bank and cover them with sand. To

which George Musgrove grumbled, "What the hell, let the buzzards have them . . . as they wouldn't bury me if the tables
had been turned."

"Use your head, George. Any sign of buzzards after something up this way will bring someone out thisaway."

"Yeah, come on, George," said Jess Williams, "and you,
too, Sixtoes, let's get it over with."

Watching all of this, Henry Thompson just kept on eating,
withdrawn as he was in some musing reverie out of his past.
He had some whiskey stowed in a saddlebag, but he wasn't
in a drinking mood. That bank job at Loma had been a sweet
deal, in and out and gone. Did he really want to help wet-nurse
these cattle up toward the Canadian line? A long haul through
those bitterly tough breaks and long days and with little sleep.
On the other side of the coin was the chance of angry cattlemen coming after them. He tossed his tin plate down and
burped as he said to Black Jack, "Maybe we should hump out
of here tonight."

"We'll leave before this night has run its course, Henry,
around three or four—an' lucky for us these cattle are still
holding in close together."

"I counted around four, five hundred head—about all we
can handle." Pulling out a cigar, Henry Thompson leaned toward the fire with the cigar in his mouth and let the flames
light it. With them were Will Christian, Bob Hays and Dunlop,
and he knew if anybody could pull this off, it was these boys.

"You got another one of those?" Hays asked.

Long Henry scowled and said, "Two things I don't loan out,
my guns and my cigars. Stick to your tailor-mades as you'll
last longer." He turned his eyes upon Sixtoes and Jess Williams
coming back to remove the last dead body. "No witnesses;
suits me right well. Now I'll be sackin' out. An' when I wake,
the man standin' killpecker guard before better have some Arbuckles waitin'." A smile etched across Thompson's face,
though those watching weren't sure if he was just joshing to
cut the sting of his words or meant it.

* * *

As promised, Black Jack Christian, calculating it was around three o'clock by the mental timepiece in his head, was up and rousing the others. The man standing the last watch turned out to be Will Christian, whose saddled horse stood tied to a nearby tree, and there was a coffeepot heating over the ember-spitting fire. He said quietly to his brother, "I rode out a ways to see how much the herd had drifted. Not all that much, so we shouldn't have any trouble forming them together and pointing them due east."

"From what Glendenning told us," said Black Jack, "the Circle W has another four thousand head of livestock. But what we take now will make a sizable dent in their herd." He took in the horses of the dead cowhands still tied under the trees. Along with the bodies, the saddles and other rigging had been buried down by the creek. They would take the horses, and once they'd had time to alter the brands, a chore that Six-toes Baker would handle, they could be resold for a nice profit.

As Will Christian kicked sand over the camp fire to douse the flames, his cohorts set about saddling their horses. That quarter moon still hung in, though it was a far piece westerly, and going on four now the sky had changed slightly to cast down a little more light. Removing the halter ropes from the other horses, they turned them loose and mounted up to haze the loose horses in the direction of the herd beginning to stir at the approach of the riders.

It took nearly an hour to form the herd to Black Jack's liking, and none of them complaining. For out here there was only room for one leader, as they could and probably would run into some kind of trouble before reaching the breaks. By sunup they were north of the Judiths and not all that far from the settlement of Marcourt, and the cattle were still moving easily. They hadn't encountered a solitary horseman, and even Henry Thompson had lost that grumpy mood and had even whistled, once.

As he was wont to do, Black Jack had sent a rider ahead to scout out the approaches to the last watering hole before they reached the breaks, and when Three-Fingered Jack pulled out of the clearing darkness he sought out Black Jack to say, "Box Elder Creek lies just beyond that lonely butte, an' all I scared up were some mule deer."

Twisting in the saddle, Black Jack looked at the herd strung out in the line of march, and he said, "This first time we came out okay; I reckon we broke our cherries so to speak up here. We won't take all that much time lettin' 'em drink, though. As once we're in the breaks I'll breathe a lot easier. Now if only them Frenchies are as good as they claim to be . . ."

NINE

Even the weather worked in favor of the High Fives, for two days later a low front shuddered in from the northwest to cast down a mingling of sleet and heavy rain onto parts of north-central Montana. To wipe out traces of their passage into the breaks. Once they had forded the Missouri, at which time they'd lost a few calfs and some steers, they drove the herd farther north boldly in daylight hours. According to Pierre LaFleur, there was only one settlement between them and the rendezvous point, the Cloud Coulee marshy area. Up front at point with Black Jack rode Long Henry.

"West of here," said Thompson, "is Fort Belknap Indian Reservation. Home of the Gros Ventres and Assiniboines. Could be some of those half bloods riding with LaFleur come from there."

"I just hope they'll be waitin' to take these cattle off our hands and not be runnin' their clocks on Indian time."

"Yeah, where a blood says he'll meet you on Monday, he really means Friday or later. But LaFleur looked steady enough, Black Jack. One thing in our favor is that two day rainstorm wiped out our back trail."

As the day wore on toward mid-afternoon, Henry Thompson, who'd ridden through these parts before, remarked, "Up along the Chinook is a place called Wishbone. Nothing but a road ranch of sorts; run by old Sol Prentice."

"We could use some liquid refreshment and smokes," said Black Jack, as his probing eyes settled in on a couple of horsemen lurking on a distant and northerly knoll. He and Thompson sawed back softly on their reins, with Thompson reaching back to take a field glass out of a saddlebag, through which he scoped in on the riders.

He muttered, "Yup, some of LaFleur's 'breeds." Now he waved the field glass over his head in a ride-on-in motion. "Eases my mind some."

"Just so LaFleur is waitin' at Black Coulee with the money."

It was already being talked about as the tragedy along Coffee Creek. The bodies had been discovered by a Circle W hand when he'd sought a sheltered spot along the creek during the recent rainstorm. Coming in, he'd scared up some turkey vultures feasting on something on the other side of the creek. At first all he could see was where the sandy bank had been dug up, with curiosity causing him to ford over, and here he sighted in on what was left of someone's upper body. Further investigation turned up more bodies, and promptly he'd jumped aboard his bronc and forked it at full gallop back to the home buildings.

In the days to follow, lawmen were summoned out, and joining them was Nick Dunn. Generally rustlers conducted hit-and-run raids, in which they might get a dozen or more cattle. Maybe a cowpuncher would get nicked by a bullet. Or a rustler would go down. Among the cowmen out by the creek was Tom Wilson, who shakily said as he stared at the five graves dotting the lonely hillside a short distance away, "This was nothing but a slaughterhouse." A grim reminder to the graves were the saddles that had been dug up and placed in a wagon bed.

Every rancher for at least thirty miles around had come to support Pete Burkel, the owner of the Circle W. One of them had read a brief eulogy over the graves of the recently demised cowpokes. Another had expressed bitterly that the next rustler he caught would die right there. All of this registered in the thoughts of stock inspector Nick Dunn, that right now if any of them had even the slightest inkling he was really a wanted high rider, he'd be skydancing from one of those cottonwoods.

That damned Glendenning, Nick Dunn mused silently. *The damn fool didn't tell me the High Fives would get into this kind of killing. What they did was issue a declaration of all-out war to the cattlemen. Maybe I should clear out and to hell with it all*

All of the ranchers, and this included a few foremen and cowpokes, had left their womenfolk behind. Right now the wind was whistling softly through the treeline and the distant tules, and the men were claiming their horses preparatory to accompanying Pete Burkel back to his place for some chow and some discussion on just how to handle all of this. One of Burkel's hands took off first driving the wagon holding the saddles and some shovels. Farther out on the reaches of ranch land it looked kind of barren without any cattle grazing about. And taking this in, Nick Dunn rode in closer to where Tom Wilson sat his horse chatting with the Circle W owner.

"Mr. Burkel, as you know I just took over this job. Still and all, I've got some idea where to find the Hayward bunch."

Tom Wilson said, "They don't operate this way, Nick."

"I know, but they could point me to the men responsible for this."

The rancher said, "Go for it, Nick. You need help, you come a'whistling."

"Thank you, Mr. Burkel, I'll do that." Quickly he reined his horse away and set it cantering to the north along the creek, only too glad to be shed of all these cattlemen. He had never felt easy around honest men, especially with all of their pious talk of how they made their fortunes. Some of them were just lucky in that they'd gotten away with some illegal acts at one time or another.

Coffee Creek and the Circle W Ranch were two days behind Nick Dunn when he set his eyes upon Dupuyer. For miles around, grassy slopes pushed up to the higher mountain peaks hidden behind a low cloud bank. One N Bar cowpoke had told him some as to how this little Indian settlement got its name. Seems back in the 1840's when butchering a buffer the shoulders were taken off, as well as the hindquarters, and the sides, covered by a thin portion of flesh called the depouille, are also cut away. The Blackfoot had corrupted the word depouille into what became known as Dupuyer.

Nick could see why outlaws would hang out here, in that their backsides were protected by tree-stippled canyons pushing toward the snowcapped peaks. Yet this was still Blackfoot country, and for the last fifty miles he'd been keeping an eye out for Indians. These Blackfeet, he knew, didn't cotton much to intruders, especially starpackers, entering their domain.

"That Hayward gang . . . they must be givin' part of what they steal to the Blackfeet. As tribute to bein' able to hang out here."

He was still a couple of miles out. He'd been coming in cross-country, simply because there were no trails fringing in from the east. By the angle of the sun it was early afternoon. Uncertainty held him on the crest of the low grassy hill, the thought that maybe a wanted poster on him was adorning a wall in one of the establishments there. And if so, he'd be welcome with no unnecessary questions being asked.

Milt Hayward had, according to what Glendenning had told him, three other men in his gang. A big enough bunch to take out those Circle W cowpokes and steal that herd of cattle. Could be they'd sold the cattle to the Blackfeet. A tribe not adverse to trafficking in stolen goods, and fierce warriors when they got the urge to go on the warpath.

As Nick Dunn studied the approaches to the hill just in case he'd been spotted, it occurred to him that out here someplace was where that stock inspector whose job he now had had been killed. Was it possible that Milt Hayward or one of his bunch had done the killing? That just perhaps Havre lawyer Glendenning had ordered this done.

"Makes sense," he muttered, deciding to check out the settlement. "Makes a lotta sense when you nail it down proper. Once I find Mr. Hayward, I'll know."

Before heading out he took his own sweet time in tightening his saddle rigging, and then he had a drink of water as he gauged his chances of running into the Hayward gang. If they had rustled that herd, they wouldn't stick around Dupuyer but head for a bigger town. The last thing he did was tuck his stock inspector's badge into the deep recesses of a Levi's pocket. Mounting up, he let the gelding set its own pace on the downslope, the prairie grass thick and high so it brushed against his legs as he rode.

Standing above the low buildings of Dupuyer were several Blackfeet tepees. Dogs came nipping at the heels of his gelding when he rode in past an open-sided blacksmith shop. There were five more buildings equally as seedy and some pole corrals. *Nope,* he mused, eyeing one of a pair of saloons in the settlement, *this is no place to celebrate a windfall.* Out front on a shaded porch hooked to the trading post sat five Blackfeet; they shot incurious glances at the newcomer. They were older men, reservation Indians, and just idling there until somebody came by to buy them a bottle.

To his surprise the Bird Saloon had behind the bar a blustery-faced white man. He had on wide suspenders over grimy red flannel underwear and a wide gap between his upper front teeth which showed sudden pleasure at Nick Dunn's appearance. Detecting movement in the dim shadows to the rear of the barroom, Nick let his eyes turn that way in a disinterested glance. Seated at a table and playing cards were three more white men—by the way they were armed, high riders. The one with red hair had to be the outlaw Red Miller. But this was no time to go over and introduce himself.

Nick Dunn looked kind of seedy himself, in that he'd deliberately neglected to shave ever since pulling out of Box Elder. And he wore his Colt .45 low and thonged down. "Just driftin' through," he muttered to the bardog as he reached amongst the change in his pocket for a couple of quarters, which he laid carefully on the soiled bar top. "Hope that's enough for a bottle . . . of that Four Roses yonder . . ."

"Barely enough," complained the man behind the bar. He put the bottle on the bar along with a shot glass that needed washing, his hands kind of grimy with dirt curled around his fingernails. "Just passin' through, huh?"

"Canada"—Nick shaped a comradely grin—"if I get lucky and get that far."

"Law on your tail?"

"Been ever since I crossed out of Wyoming. But I figure I shook 'em up north of the Absarokas." He eyed the tray down at the end of the bar and the bottle flys buzzing around some dried food. "That the best this place can do . . ."

"I could muster up some more grub—but not for no four bits, mister."

"Way it is," alibied Nick. "Can anybody get into that game?"

The bardog didn't respond to this, but a man at the table did, as he drawled out, "Yup, as it's deader around here than a cornbread fart." There was no humor in his words.

He brought the bottle along to the table and stood there for a moment under the scrutinizing eyes of the four outlaws. In him though was a calmness, since he'd now determined that the red-haired man matched the drawing on one of his wanted posters. *The way it is,* Nick mused, *you're looking for a certain bunch and you run into others on your wanted list.*

"You from Kansas?"

"Nope," said Nick, as he dragged a chair over.

"At least that's where I saw your picture . . . Mr. Starky True."

He stared back at the outlaw, a mean-mouthed man with a drooping handlebar mustache and whose coat lay open to reveal the pair of sixguns. Sooner or later the moment of truth would come for him, but he didn't expect it to happen in a place like Dupuyer, which was about as far as you could get from civilization without going over the edge. "So, I look like this outlaw True. You could be Buffalo Bill Cody for all I know."

The red-haired man laughed. "Don't mind Alvin none. One thing though, he has a damned good memory about such things. Just what is your handle, stranger?"

The air still reeked with suspense, even though smiles appeared. And now Nick Dunn caught a glimpse of the gun one of the outlaws was holding in his lap underneath the table. Carefully Nick reached for the folded jackknife he kept in a vest pocket. "Just what has this Starky True done?"

"A mean, murderin' son'bitch," one of the outlaws said where he sat riffling the deck of cards. "Heard he killed five men down in Wyoming."

Holding the jackknife in the palm of his hand so they could see it, Nick directed his words at the red-haired man. "No Blackfoot that I've ever heard of has red hair. So you must be Red Miller . . ." Now the smiles at the table evaporated, and Nick Dunn added calmly, "Got my name etched into the blade of this jackknife." He tossed it at Miller, who caught the knife and pulled the blade out.

"I'll be damned—you really are Starky True. Fold onto that chair, Mr. True. Here, Waldo, sell the illustrious Mr. True some chips. It ain't much of a game; dollar limit."

"Rich enough for me," said Nick, upon easing onto the chair and taking a swig from his bottle. "What kind of law they got here?"

"Ain't got none—reason we're holding in here. Just some dumb Indians, and some squaws if you're so inclined."

"How far to the border?"

"On a fast hoss less'n a day." His voice was slurred, and with unsteady hands he picked up the cards tossed in front of him by the dealer.

As he got into the game, Nick Dunn could pick out the telltale signs that these men had been hunkered in here for at least a couple of days, pouring down corn whiskey and probably taking a break from the game to visit the squaws. The Hayward gang would have to play second fiddle now that these men knew who he was. With the afternoon wearing on into dusk, a plan came to him, in that Red Miller had revealed he had a hideout camp up west of here in a canyon. The fact they knew he was Starky True prompted a quick invite from the outlaws to hook up with them. And just as promptly he accepted.

"When we rustle cattle," complained Red Miller, "we have to give these greedy Indians a share. You mentioned, Starky, this big cattle sale over at Brady . . ."

"Yup, some old-time rancher had everything he owned auctioned off. I was there during the sale. Took in a heap of money. Which that rancher deposited in that tinny bank over at Brady. Should be easy pickings, Red, if we do it right."

"At least we won't have to pay these Indians anything, Starky. We could pull out for Brady in the morning."

"You figure your men'll be sobered up by then."

"Yeah, what the hell, it's goin' on midnight. Okay, buy what booze you want as we're cuttin' out for camp."

Nearly an hour and a half later the outlaws and Nick Dunn were coming in slowly along the rising floor of a canyon. They were following a worn trail pushing through thick stands of fir trees, the pine smell wafting around them, until finally the trail widened to reveal a small meadow and a log cabin. One of the outlaws was still whistling away, tuneless, probably just to keep himself awake so that he wouldn't fall out of the saddle. As they rode, they'd been sucking from whiskey bottles, a way of life that would soon eat their livers away if a bullet didn't kill them first.

"Corral's back of the cabin, Starky." Twisting in the saddle, Red Miller added loudly, "Be sure and take care of your hosses before you hit the sack, dammit. As we'll be ridin' hot and heavy for Brady come sunup."

"We ain't comin' back here, are we, Red?"

"Hell, no, let's try holin' up around Sun River after we pull this bank job." Red Miller led the way around to the back of the cabin, where everyone swung down under moonlight, or what there was of it filtering through the fir trees. The air was dead still, as was the case in these deep mountain canyons. Distantly an owl cut loose in a mournful hunting song.

Now that he was here, Nick Dunn copied everyone else as he unsaddled his bronc and turned it loose in the corral. The cabin, he'd noticed, only had one room. Which meant that some of these men would probably sleep outside in their bedrolls. It wasn't long before two of the outlaws stumbled into the cabin, and Nick was bedding down close to the others along the north wall of the cabin and under screening fir branches. No sooner, it seemed, had the outlaws crawled into their bedrolls than they were snoring drunkenly.

Nick Dunn held to his bedroll for a couple of hours, needing the rest. One of the horses in the corral was restless, whickering at times and stomping around a bit, but it didn't disturb the outlaws still gripped in a dead sleep. And now Nick rose to roll up his bedding and make his way back to the corral. Carefully he found his horse and brought it out of the corral, where in the darkness of night he managed to cinch the saddle into place. He brought another horse out and tethered it close to his.

Out again came his sharp jackknife, for he saw no way out of what he was about to do next. These men had signed their death warrants when his name had come up back at Dupuyer. *I bring them in . . . they'll sure as hell tell everyone I'm Starky True. Can't afford to let them go either. Nor can I afford to feel remorseful about this . . . as they'd do the same to me . . .*

First he eased back to come in on the men snoring away under the fir tree. Then he brought his jackknife cutting deeply across the throat of the first man, who just went limp as he died. He did the same to the second outlaw, pausing to brush the blade of his knife across the shirt of the dead man to rid it of some blood.

Easing inside the cabin, Nick waited for a moment as a thought came to him. The big reward money was out on Red Miller, dead or alive. But surely questions would be asked of him if he brought Miller's body in with the man's throat cut wide open. He could hear their heavy breathing as he came in on the pair of bunks sitting side by side past the potbellied stove. He disposed of the outlaw, Alvin, same as he did the men outside, with one strong cutting stroke of his jackknife. Carefully he wiped the blood from the blade before he folded the knife and put it away. Unleathering his Colt, he reversed his grip on the gun and slammed the butt end down on Red Miller's left temple.

Now that he was in control of the situation, Nick Dunn got a lamp going, and a fire in the potbellied stove. Almost casually he set about frying a slab of bacon in a big black-encrusted frying pan, the coffee he'd made starting to perk. He found some spuds, peeled a couple and threw them piecemeal into the pan with the bacon. There was some whiskey, but he ignored the bottles, something he wouldn't have done a few years ago. But he was older, wiser, a dried-out man in his late thirties, to whom caution and patience were his only friends. At least they wouldn't shoot him in the back.

It did occur to Nick upon pulling out just after sunup to bury the dead outlaws. But he had brushed this aside, and instead, he had lifted Red Miller still alive aboard his horse and tied him belly down, with the man receiving another rap on the head from the butt of Nick's sixgun. The rest of the plan was to strike out for Shelby. This was where stock inspector Poul Gregson had succumbed to his wounds received from the guns of the Hayward gang. Right now folks up there, and lawmen, would be more than eager to make the acquaintance of any outlaw. And Nick aimed to oblige them by delivering Red Miller. Out of this he would gain a new measure of credibility with the ranchers.

The route Nick Dunn took was a few miles east of the stagecoach road running up to Shelby. The second day out he let Red Miller sit up in his saddle, though Miller was still tied up. As yet, he hadn't revealed to Miller that his gang was no more, and with Nick about to do just that, he removed the cigarillo from between his clenched teeth. He'd pinned the stock inspector's badge to his vest, the bitter rage of Red Miller taking that in, as Miller spat out, "You sneaky rat. . . . wait 'til my boys catch up to us . . ."

"Won't happen in your lifetime, Red—nor theirs."

"What's that supposed to mean?"

Nick didn't respond to the question as he yanked on the halter rope he was holding. The outlaw's horse and Nick's broke into a lope that brought them toward some screening rocks lying near the lower reaches of a butte. In amongst the rocks, Nick stared to the northwest at a small dust cloud made by several riders. From the way they rode he knew they were Blackfeet, though they were at least a mile and a half away. He held there, watching them recede into the distance. Any one of them might be acquainted with his prisoner, and then he'd be the one roped to his saddle.

He reached down to remove the canteen strap from his saddle horn. Before taking a sip, he said, "We're not all that far from Shelby, Mr. Miller."

Red Miller snapped back, "You was about to tell me somethin' about my boys . . . so spit it out, damn you, Starky True."

"Just that they've cashed in their chips, Red."

"You murderin' devil! When I get to Shelby I'm spillin' the beans about you, True, damn your hide . . ."

"Shelby—you'll get there all right." Casually Nick drew his Colt. He thumbed the hammer back, grinning into the face of Red Miller suddenly gone slack with fear. "But strung belly down dead over your saddle." His gun bucked, and the slug from it tore into the outlaw's gaping mouth to come out the back of his head. The fact his hands were tied close to the horn of his saddle and another rope looped under the belly of his horse and around his booted ankles kept the dead outlaw saddlebound.

Swinging down, Nick took another sip from the canteen before corking it and tying the strap to his saddle horn. There was a tug at the halter rope he held, the outlaw's horse starting to tremble more now that it caught the scent of blood. "Easy, boy . . . easy . . ." He worked his way back along the rope and patted the gelding on the forehead. Walking the horse over to a nearby limber pine, he then tied the rope around the trunk and set about unfastening the dead rustler. It took some effort, but he managed to swing the body so it lay draped over the back of the horse, and then he retied the ropes.

Shelby, he found, was a large, pleasant-looking town located about twenty miles north of the Marias River. A horseman came in off a side street and swung in behind Nick Dunn as he was clearing the shade of some trees and passing in front of a mercantile store. Others took notice of the intruder as Nick rode past a freight wagon, and then some cowhands who'd just left a saloon watched him rein up before the sheriff's office. The man coming out of the building took in the badge pinned to Nick Dunn's vest; then he came off the boardwalk and stared into the face of the dead outlaw.

"I'll be damned—that's Red Miller?"

Nick untied one of his saddlebags, which he took with him into the stone-walled building, the sheriff following to go behind his desk as the contents of Nick's saddlebag, four sixguns, clattered onto the desktop.

"Miller's gun is there along with those belonging to that bunch he rode with."

"You mean . . . they're all dead . . ." Skepticism played across the sheriff's face. "You're that new man workin' for the stockman's association . . . Nick Dunn. Now you ride in here expectin' me to believe you took 'em all out . . ."

"I did," Nick said flintily. "Now you just make up them papers citing I'm to get that reward out on Red Miller, and maybe those others. Here, jot down their names, too . . ."

"Reckon so," the sheriff said with slowly diminishing disbelief. "Seems, Mr. Dunn, they picked the right man for the job."

TEN

N Bar N foreman Tom Wilson's reason for going into Box Elder was to leave notice he was hiring. Tom felt, as did his fellow cattlemen, that more men were needed to help protect their herds from this onslaught of rustling. There was even talk of importing gunhands. While some cowmen were telling their congressmen to send out army units to help in this killing war ripping throughout north-central Montana.

Tom's biggest worry was just simply that of going into town. Within the last week two of his closest neighbors had been hit, and more men killed. He was astride his big, rangy bay stallion. Until a year ago the bay had run wild, and even now it would revert back to its wild ways by rearing up occasionally. Tom knew that if he turned the stallion loose, it would find another band of mares. He'd left it corraled during spring branding, had used it after that during the short haying season and to go out on the range to check on his cowpokes. The stallion had sired several colts, and he hoped to have more before he turned it out to pasture.

Closing in now on Box Elder, one of his other reasons for making this long ride came flooding in. He just wanted to see Vivian McCauley. Hadn't done so too many times over a long winter scarcely over. The more he mused on it now, the more he realized his inattention toward Vivian could have sent a message he wasn't interested. "But she knows how I feel . . . though I haven't told her in so many words . . ." The fact that the last time he'd seen Vivian it had been with Nick Dunn spurred not only Tom's concerns but had him urging his horse into a lope.

One other thing was something he couldn't put off any longer, that being a palaver with Ralph Glendenning. Decisions had to be made about the N Bar, fixing up some of the buildings and either selling off some livestock or buying more land. The sorry thing of this whole deal was that the absentee owners let Glendenning control the purse strings. Tom suspected that the lawyer was spending the money for other purposes, along with sticking it to the owners with some high legal bills. "Lawyers—worst thing the Good Lord ever created."

Just coming into Box Elder felt good to Tom, seeing not only houses and such, but folks he knew passing along the street. Memories of some good times jogged at him as he tightened his grip on the reins to calm the stallion, which was getting jittery over things it hadn't seen before and the undercurrent noises spilling about. The livery doors were open, and he rode in instead of dismounting outside. The sight of other horses settled the stallion down.

"Hey there, Tom Wilson, thought you forgot all about us common folks."

"Charley, how do," he returned as he climbed down and led his horse into an empty stall. "I wouldn't stand behind this hammerhead, Charley, as you never know. You're lookin' fit."

"For an old fart, yeah. You boys been hit by these rustlers yet?"

"Nope," he said tautly. He removed the saddle and draped it over a stall rail. Going up to the front doors, they exchanged small talk, and then Tom left to turn the corner and make for the Commercial Bank, where he wanted to make sure that Glendenning had deposited money to pay for operating expenses and wages due his cowpokes. Closing in on the bank, he took a quick gander upstreet at the Carbine Hotel. In the past he'd always gotten a room farther along at the Roadway House, but with Vivian managing the Carbine it sure changed things.

Another change, Tom soon found upon entering the bank, was that the bank's owner, Bobby Trousdale, had retired. You could always count upon Bobby, a fiery, short-bodied man, to give you some sage advice on saving money and a *"do you really need this loan"* sermon. One thing, though, about the Commercial, it was the most solvent bank in Montana. Now a teller directed Tom toward the banker's old office, which, Tom found, was being presided over by new bank president Otto Vetter. There was planted on the teller's face a masked look, which he didn't think too much about at the moment, a kind of grimace usually reserved for viewing a dead body or when encountering some undesirable.

"Been a while, Tom."

"Yup, Otto, so you're runnin' things now." He didn't bother with removing his hat as he lowered onto the chair in front of the desk.

"I don't know how to tell you this, Tom . . ."

"Maybe your teller has," he cut in. "In that Mr. Glendenning hasn't deposited any money."

"There's some, Tom. A couple of hundred and change. He did send some money down last week. But only after we sent up several letters."

"So how do we stand, Otto?"

"First of all, Tom, we're not questioning your credibility. I know that Glendenning has let you run things out at the N Bar, and make the decisions about culling out stock and selling them during fall roundup. If I were you, Tom, I'd contact the owners and lay it out for them. Tell them, too, Tom, that we'd be willing to help in any way we could. Spelling it out further, I feel that Glendenning is stealing you blind."

"I know he gambles a lot," said Tom. "The N Bar is one of the best spreads around; plenty of water and cover. Pity it went under because of this. This only firms up my intentions to head up to Havre. I'll need to have supplies sent out . . . and if I don't pay my hands . . . Tell you what, Otto, I've got some savings in my account here; goin' on three thousand. Transfer a couple of thousand to the N Bar account and—"

"No, Tom, I won't do that."

Though confusion played across his face, he remained silent as Otto Vetter said, "We'll just loan the N Bar the two thousand. You go ahead and make up a list of what you need for the ranch and how much money you need to met your payroll. I'll have the supplies wagoned out while you're up in Havre."

"Otto, this sets my mind a lot easier. Like you said, this monkeyshine business with Glendenning has gone on long enough. I've sent reports to him as to cattle sales and expenses. At the same time I've got a second set of books snookered away. If he's been stealing N Bar money, he's lawyer enough to try and pin it on someone else. I owe you for your support, Otto."

"Box Elder needs the N Bar and men like you, Mr. Wilson, as neighbors."

"You know, Bobby Trousdale would have done the same thing."

"Knew you'd be in before long, Tom. Had a board meeting the other night, at which time we all agreed, Bobby included, to support the N Bar as long as you're segundo out there. See you in church, Tom."

"Or at Bertie's, as I sure owe you a drink."

After leaving the bank, Tom Wilson took a walk over to the Joslin & Hubbard Express office to check on the next stage for Havre. He would have ridden the stallion up there, but considering how spooked it had gotten in smaller Box Elder, Tom knew a stage would be safer and a lot more comfortable. Purchasing a ticket for the morning's stage, he went on to check into the Carbine Hotel.

The only one in the lobby was the clerk. The wall clock, and also the rumble coming from his stomach, told Tom it was noon. He left his saddlebags with the clerk, but bashfully refrained from asking about Vivian McCauley. The scent of new paint came to him, the lobby showing other signs of having been redecorated, and summery curtains had been hung to replace the old red ones. Like a woman, he mused idly, to make everything over. From here he found the dining room—anxiously, though he tried to hide it, his eyes looked about for Vivian.

Instead a wave from town marshal Parker Dillingham brought him over to the man's table by one of the windows. As befitted his heft, Dillingham seemed to be actually occupying two chairs. He didn't mind people poking fun at the fact he was overweight. That times had changed was evident in that now the marshal was packing a gunbelt. Along with some plates the bowls on the table held mashed potatoes, gravy, and greens, and there was a meat platter and a remaining t-bone steak, which now fell prey to Dillingham's fork. With barely concealed amusement Tom eyed a small plate holding the bones from two other t-bones that the marshal had eaten.

"Parker, you're a legend in your own time."

"Just a little to tide me over until supper, Tom. Hey, I got this here letter from chief stock inspector Billy Smith. I sent Billy a letter tellin' him how Nick Dunn took out the Red Miller gang. Says in the letter here that he's never met Dunn, and to tell Nick Dunn to keep up the good work. And—P.S.— Billy says here he might stop at Box Elder on his way to Havre . . . as he has to testify at a trial up there."

A twinge of jealousy struck into Tom Wilson, for the last time he'd been here it was to find Vivian being escorted around town by Dunn, and he said, "Is Nick in town?"

"Was here for a couple of days—then he took off someplace."

The waitress came up to take Tom's order, and as he told her what he wanted, Marshal Dillingham said for dessert he wanted a couple of wedges of blueberry pie. "Land sakes," the waitress said, "Parker, one day you're gonna just explode."

"Is she on your case again?" asked Vivian, who'd just come

into the dining room through a side door, with her eyes going questioningly to Tom Wilson as he came to his feet. He pulled out a chair for her, and they both settled down. "You're looking good, Tom."

"Just like a nice hunk of beefsteak, if you marble it down and let it age for a while, it just gets better. I like that dress." He smiled at the blue satiny dress molded to her full body.

"You cowboys are all the same; you hang out at the ranch so long that when you do come in everything looks a heap better. But, thank you, Mr. Wilson. As for our town marshal, his eating habits are breaking the town treasury."

"Shucks, Viv, a man's gotta keep his strength up."

Through the smile contained in her eyes was this glimmer of concern. It could be some rustlers might come into Box Elder, and this would surely place Parker Dillingham in danger, because he was no gunhand to speak of. And there was Tom, as stolid and handsome as they come, the fact being that it would be his responsibility to face up to these rustlers if they hit the N Bar. And it could happen, for to mind came the barbaric way those Circle W cowpokes had been slaughtered. She did like Tom, probably more than she should. But getting him to evidence more interest in her without being too obvious about it, well, she was just plumb good and tired of waiting for him to make his move. Then Nick Dunn had come along, to further confuse her thoughts. Either man would make a fine husband. But why should the pair of them want to marry someone getting on into her thirties. She let this drift, responding to a question from Tom with a smile that revealed the even rows of her teeth. "Tonight, you know I'd love to have supper with you, Tom."

Other men, knowing she'd been seeing Nick Dunn, would probably have asked if this would be all right with Nick. But not courtly Tom Wilson, and this was probably why he had secured a place in her heart.

That evening, after an afternoon spent calling on some old friends, and also of supervising the gathering together of what supplies they needed out at the ranch, Tom came out of his second-floor room in the Carbine Hotel and went downstairs. The new outfit he'd purchased of Levi's, a dark blue shirt, and a new string tie, gave him a feeling of ease as he sauntered into the barroom to jaw with some locals while waiting for Vivian to put in an appearance.

The place wasn't all that crowded, and the talk was subdued, for the tragedy out at the Circle W still dominated everyone's thoughts. He drank his whiskey neat, then set the shot glass down to order a refill, as merchant Stan Tyler said to him, "We just simply don't have enough lawmen our there, Tom. Nick Dunn can't do it all. There's the county sheriff . . . but you can discount our town marshal—the big tub of lard."

"For a truth Parker is hefty. But he's just that, Mr. Tyler, underpaid and pretty much untrained to be a regular lawman. You want a gunhand; you'll have to fork over some big money. Besides"—there was an edge to Tom's voice—"rustlers hit where the cattle are. Meaning you merchants are in no danger." Downing the whiskey, he spun away and pushed into the lobby just as Vivian came into it, and they headed out the front door.

"You look nettled."

"Just defendin' Parker from his detractors. Nice, isn't it?"

Hooking her arm through his, Vivian sighed her agreement. The sky was dulling and a breeze sang through the trees. The street was still alive with people doing business in a place where everybody was acquainted, and sometimes, too, minded other's business, the common curse of small cowtowns, he reckoned. No thanks, he'd stick out at some ranch when he got older or try a bigger place. Just the same, he liked Box Elder. And the woman he was squiring to supper.

"Nick Dunn told me he liked working out at the N Bar."

"Is that right?"

"He seems different, somehow," Vivian said. "You can't pry much out of Nick."

"Do you like him?"

She gazed up into Tom's eyes. "I'm not sure, Tom. He's more a man of mystery than you are."

"Am I that hard to figure out," he threw back as he opened the door to the cafe.

"Sometimes, Mr. Wilson, you are. But, oh, it's good to see you again."

The stagecoach had pulled out around nine o'clock on the twenty-odd mile run to Havre, making it the noon dinner hour when Tom Wilson arrived at Ralph Glendenning's office on Madison Street. There was no sign on the locked door to indicate where Glendenning had gone. As he pondered over this, Tom chided himself for not firing up a telegram. From here he went to one of his old haunts, the River Bend casino, to partake of a light noon lunch washed down with a stein of cold beer. He'd managed to get a table out on the veranda looking down at the Milk River. He didn't tary, but paid his bill and went back to Madison Street.

Impatiently he gazed through the door pane into the dark office. It was going on two o'clock as Tom sorted through the places where the lawyer could be, the courthouse or most likely at one of the casinos. This was one of the things he didn't like about Ralph Glendenning, just how careless the man could be when gambling. *When you're gamblin' other people's money away what difference does it make? Man don't give a hoot if my 'pokes get paid, it seems.*

Out in front of the building, which housed other businesses, Tom's shaded eyes speared upstreet to the main boulevard where traffic was thicker. He could go over to the Homestead Bank just to see if Glendenning still had an account there; a foolish notion, he decided. His plans at present were to catch the late afternoon stage back to Box Elder. "Just have to check the bars and gaming joints," Tom muttered, as he set his long legs into motion on the planking making up this section of boardwalk.

And as Tom Wilson pushed along toward Coolidge Boulevard, a man came out of a building across the street and moved along at a slower gait while sizing up the cattleman who'd just been up to see Ralph Glendenning. He was a deputy U.S. marshal, Harlow Bennett by name, and onto his first good lead into those behind all of this rustling of late. Only yesterday had Bennett and Canadian Mountie Doug McCray arrived here after tracking one of their prime suspects down through the southern reaches of Saskatchewan and here to Havre.

At the moment McCray was wandering around town in the guise of a cowpuncher trying to locate Pierre LaFleur. Last night LaFleur had given them the slip, up about ten miles north of the Milk River. Bennett's reasoning was that if LaFleur had spotted them, he wouldn't be hanging around Havre. But Marshal Harlow Bennett felt the man was still here, because of the events taking place during a recent gunfight between outlaws and lawmen up at Swift Current. One of the outlaws they'd captured had implicated LaFleur, stating that the man was hooked up with a Havre lawyer. They weren't even sure this was Ralph Glendenning, even though the town marshal had hinted at this, with Marshal Bennett concluding this was only petty spite. The fact Glendenning hadn't been in his office today, or at any of his usual haunts, could be coincidental. But capturing criminals was pretty much like going fishing, mused Harlow Bennett, in that you didn't catch all the fish in a trout stream. But they had one now, it seemed, that big cowboy ambling along the opposite side of the street.

"Went up twice lookin' for this lawyer. Seemed kind of agitated when he came down that second time. Should hold back there watchin' the lawyer's office as both he and McCray might come wanderin' back . . . but this cowpoke interests me . . ."

You could tell Harlow Bennett was a chain-smoker by the yellowed stain on the tips of his fingers setting the hand-rolled between his teeth. He was thirty, and all he'd ever wanted was to be a lawman like his pa and grandpappy before that. There wasn't a spare ounce of fat on his wiry frame of around five-ten, and he was dressed similar to the man he was following, though he wore black trousers instead of Levi's. He no longer measured the territory he covered in miles but in days, in how many days it took to get to such and such a place or yonder. The more vicious criminal element knew this, and acted accordingly. So catching them was getting harder, but a man had to keep trying.

And why should a man who argued cases before a court of law turn outlaw himself? Was it just a case of Pierre LaFleur using this lawyer as a money drop? That Ralph Glendenning, or some other Havre lawyer, was merely an unwitting pawn in this rustling game? These were questions that had to be considered first of all, for if this was a dead lead, it would be damned foolish watching Glendenning's office while LaFleur hooked up with these rustlers again.

At least the Red Miller gang was out of the picture, Bennett mused, as the man he was following entered the Lady Bird Gambling Emporium. This stock inspector, Nick Dunn, must be hell on wheels to be able to take out four men. And still the rustling went on. They had discussed, him and Mountie Doug McCray, going after the Hayward gang. Most likely, though, some cattlemen would get there first and kill all of those outlaws. But Bennett doubted that bunch was behind these killings. Milt Hayward may be a high ridin' rustler, but he was no cold-blooded killer. He'd thrown Milt into the clink more times than he cared to remember, disorderly and drunk, petty theft, once for a stagecoach job, but never for murder. Before pulling out of Lewistown for the boonies, he'd fired off some wires inquiring about certain known cattle rustlers, fearing that a lot of them had drifted up into Montana.

He went into the casino and soon exited to tail the lanky cattleman pushing into other gaming places and saloons. He was hoping he'd run into McCray, who might be having better luck. As walking in high-heeled boots was wearing on his feet.

* * *

"I told you that packing plant up there paid up front . . . and top dollar for every head we can deliver."

"Everything went smoothly—"

"They are professionals, these High Fives," replied Pierre LaFleur. They were in one of the back gambling rooms at the Four Aces casino. He smiled at Glendenning riffling through a thick sheaf of greenbacks. The open saddlebag contained another thousand dollars, out of which the Canuck had taken his share.

"What about Black Jack, did he head back into the breaks?"

"I'm not his keeper, Ralph. And if they do stop along the way to do a little celebrating, it will be done quietly at some road ranch. As Black Jack told me, there's time to play and also time to work. The way this setup is, that means pushing out to hit another herd of cattle. This new man of his, Long Henry, has some thoughts on this. Anyway, when I leave here I'm hooking up with Black Jack down at Box Elder to iron out this new route."

"Henry . . . Thompson?"

LaFleur nodded as he lifted the stein of beer.

Glendenning remembered that Long Henry worked out at the N Bar. And there was something else that tugged at his mind, which he let slip away as he ran a comforting hand over the money he held before he replaced the greenbacks in the saddlebag and buckled the flap.

"Rehashing it before we go, Pierre, the High Fives have hit three ranches. Leaving a lot of dead men behind. To this end I've been invited to a meeting of my fellow ranchers, shall we say, the purpose being to form a vigilante committee."

"I expected this." LaFleur shrugged. "This time Black Jack will hit way over by the Rockies—at least a hundred and fifty miles from the last ranch he raided. While the ranchers are riding around in circles someplace else." His low, mocking laughter lifted past cigar smoke tainting the air to pass out an open window. "There are rustlers—and then there are the High Fives. It is good to be working with the best."

"I hope so," Glendenning said with just a tinge of worry. Refilling his glass from the whiskey bottle, he shifted his thoughts to a nagging problem in the form of Tom Wilson, his foreman out at the N Bar. By now Wilson must have figured out that he was stealing money sent by the absentee owners. He should have sent more money down to the bank in Box Elder, had planned to do so, but gambling and women had interfered. He'd be pulling out anyway, in the fall, but until then he would have to contend with foreman Wilson.

"The N Bar," he said, "yes, I want that ranch hit next."

"Hit your own spread? You sure?"

"Yes, definitely, Pierre. An extra thousand to the man that kills Tom Wilson. With him out of the way I have one less worry." Now he detailed to LaFleur where the cattle were being grazed and how they were guarded. "Wilson likes to go out and check on his men. Long Henry knows what Wilson looks like . . . so get the job done . . ."

Heaving up from the chair, Pierre LaFleur said, "There is still some sunlight left, and it isn't all that far to Box Elder. *Oui,* this Tom Wilson will be taken care of." He went out into the back corridor and found the back door.

All of a sudden the foul mood fled from Ralph Glendenning, for he had a saddlebag full of money, and more in the offing. Once Wilson was out of the way, his next move would be to go out to the N Bar and destroy any incriminating ledgers and papers. He could put in an interim foreman, maybe one of Black Jack's men. He could write to the owners telling of Wilson's untimely death and that most of the cattle had been rustled. Most likely they would sell out at rock-bottom prices to him. Later on, he could sell the N Bar and make a handsome profit.

"Yes, what I'll do." They had been drinking steadily at another saloon before coming here for a private talk, and the whiskey had taken hold, although he was still in control of himself. He would go to the bank and put this money into a safe deposit box, then go to his hotel suite and freshen up before making a night of it.

He left the room, but sought the main gaming room, and wished he hadn't when he found the last man he wanted to see detaching himself from the bar. Tom Wilson stepped around the roulette wheel, which was seeing some action, and came toward the lawyer, gesturing toward an empty table. "Tom, I had planned on going down to Box Elder tomorrow, to bank some money." The smile was as empty as his words. "And I apologize for not tending to business out there at the N Bar. But I just finished with one court case and got another coming up." He sat down and lowered the saddlebag to the floor.

"Well, I'm here," Tom said crisply. "Until fall there won't be any money coming in." Displeasure gritted out of his eyes when he realized that Glendenning was about two drinks shy from being totally drunk. "I want five thousand on the barrel, Ralph. Another two thousand within the week."

"You're just the foreman, Wilson. I'll pay you—"

"I'm runnin' the whole show out there. You're not worth a nickel of the money they're payin' you. I can't recall the last time you came out to check on things."

"I admit, Tom," he said pleasantly, "what you're saying is all too true. The banks are closed now. But tomorrow morning you'll have the money you need to run things and pay your men. Would you care for a drink?"

Shoving to his feet, Tom said bitterly, "I'll be at your offices at eight o'clock sharp; you be there an' we'll go over to your bank." He left Glendenning sitting at the table. Once he had the money and got back to Box Elder, he had every intention of dropping a line to the absentee owners. After that, if they didn't get rid of the lawyer, they'd be looking for a new ranch foreman. He was tired of fighting the greedy machinations of Ralph Glendenning.

From where he stood at the bar, Marshal Harlow Bennett had overheard the angry talk between the two men. He watched Tom Wilson go out the front door, his eyes going back to the lawyer picking up the saddlebags, and when Glendenning left, so did Bennett. *Could be that McCray has found this Canuck, LaFleur. As for this lawyer, the man's involved in something, an' with any luck we'll find out.*

He followed Ralph Glendenning back to the lawyer's office, and after Glendenning had gone into the building, the marshal crossed over and to his relief found Canadian Mountie Doug McCray had just gotten back. McCray was a large, broad-shouldered man whose wide face was creased with displeasure. He said, "Not a trace of LaFleur."

"I don't know if lawyer Glendenning is involved in this," said Bennett. "But I got a gut feeling he is. So that leaves us where, Doug? Those reports forwarded to me state these rustlers must have a hideout down in the Missouri Breaks. The cattle they rustle they herd north until LaFleur and his men take over."

"LaFleur could be on his way down to see these men."

"My guess. This lawyer, Glendenning, had a run-in with some cattleman. Back there I had a choice of following one or the other man. But if we run into this Tom Wilson tonight, he could answer some of our questions."

"Do you think Wilson's part of this?"

"The only thing I know right now, Doug, is that it's suppertime and the U.S. government is buying."

"And then afterward, Harlow, the Canadian government will spring for the drinks."

ELEVEN

Earlier that same afternoon a tired Nick Dunn had returned to Box Elder, and to a hero's welcome. The story of how he'd captured the Red Miller gang had spread throughout the territory. After leaving Shelby, Nick had scoured out possible hiding places in his search for Milt Hayward, to no avail, and he'd ridden off to secure lodging at some welcoming ranches on his way back here.

Now as Nick toyed with his shot glass where he sat alone at a table in the Longhorn Bar, he was thinking of how eager Glendenning was to have Milt Hayward out of the way. So he killed Hayward? Then, Nick knew, he'd be the only one left alive to know of the lawyer's connection to these crimes. The fact Glendenning knew he was Starky True also lay festering in his mind. There was danger to him in all of this. Supposing when he did find rustler Hayward, he made a deal with the man. Out of this he could blackmail the arrogant Ralph Glendenning. After all, it was Glendenning who'd set into motion all of these killings.

A smile lacing across his face, he could just picture Glendenning being forced up the steps of a gallows, the hangman there just itching to get at it, and lawmen holding on to the snivelling bastard bubbling out his protestations of pure innocence. *I know I'm a no-account gunslinger . . . on the run from a lot of crimes. But men like Glendenning. You call them thieves and they get mad as hell . . . amoral bastards . . .*

"Mr. Dunn, mind if me and Curly Parker buy you a drink . . ."

"Oh, sorry, I was . . . daydreaming. Sure, pull up a chair. What ranch do you boys work at?"

"The Stringer spread up northeast of here." Eagerly the waddy lowered onto a chair and added that his name was Lefty Bell. "We heard about how you took out them high riders, Mr. Dunn. Took out the whole bunch, we heard."

"Something like that." Amusement flared in Nick's eyes, and he found that he enjoyed their refreshing mannerisms instead of earlier when some fawning merchants had cornered him over in the dining room at the Carbine Hotel. In a way he liked the sudden notoriety, though.

A few minutes later another cowhand came into the saloon, to amble over and join them. Then one of them, Bell, got a deck of pinochle cards, and before Nick Dunn knew it, he was involved in a four-handed game of cutthroat pinochle. Time passed, and they drank, and cussed at bad hands, and Nick found himself relaxing in the ambiance of this and eye-burning smoke. It was around four, and traffic in the saloon had picked up, when a suited man wearing a bowler hat struggled through the batwings loaded down with a camera and tripod and other apparatus. Nick Dunn's table was pointed out to this worthy, who came over with an eager smile.

"Mr. Dunn . . . my, I've been trying to track you down. Rode all the way over from Shelby just to see the man who took out the Red Miller gang. Would you be so kind as to pose for some pictures?"

Concealing his displeasure as best he could, Nick tried to come up with a courteous way to tell this meddling picture taker to get the hell out of here. And then Curly Parker guffawed excitedly and said, "Sure, me and my pals would consider it a privilege to have our pictures taken alongside the famous Mr. Nick Dunn."

"Yup, Nick," threw in Lefty Bell, as oiled up with liquor

as the other card players, and like them, waiting eagerly for Stock Inspector Dunn's answer.

"Reckon it'll be okay," Nick finally said. One picture, he mused, wouldn't hurt any.

The whole thing was finally arranged, Nick Dunn and the cowhands standing in front of the ornately carved bar, and peering into the lens of the big box camera. After three pictures were taken, and with the cameraman promising to deliver the processed pictures that evening, the pinochle game resumed, with Nick wondering if he had made a mistake by letting this happen.

"Your deal, Nick."

". . . Yeah . . . sure."

A small group of men were making their way toward Box Elder, guiding around the Bearpaw Mountains. Away to the southwest lay Centennial Lookout, part of this range, and east a little bit Camels Back pushed its blunted heights against the late afternoon sky. Their guide was Long Henry Thompson, who ever since pulling across the Missouri River had been tautly silent. A large hunk of the Bearpaws, he knew, had been deeded over to form Rocky Boys Reservation, to make a home for Cree and Chippewa Indians.

He didn't feel it was necessary to detail this to Black Jack Christian loping alongside or the other High Fives. Another sore point with Long Henry was that once they left Box Elder, they faced a long ride westerly. Right now he was flush, a little tired out from the strain of not only rustling these herds, but afterward the chore of getting them up to the Canucks.

"So far we've been lucky."

Black Jack replied, "Thought you lost your tongue, Henry. Lucky—not when you hit them hot and heavy, as we've been doing. Hit and run, hit and run." As a lesser elevation fell behind, he could see scrub trees marking Box Elder Creek. "I know you're pissed about havin' to head clear over to just this side of the Rockies. We can't keep playin' a pat hand like this."

"I know, the ranchers around here are really watchin' their cattle." He bit into the hunk of chewing tobacco. He let it get settled in his mouth, chewing on it and gumming it around, the flavor of it tangy sharp in his mouth and nostrils. When he spat out juice, some of it trickled onto the shoulders of his bronc. "Before we pull out to the west more, I'd sure like to hit the N Bar N, and waste some old ridin' comrades . . . especially that Nick Dunn. What say we tackle that spread next—"

"We could," speculated Black Jack, as through the spreading haze of twilight he could see the town of Box Elder still a half-hour ride away. "We'll see what Pierre LaFleur has to say."

"That Frenchy don't give a hoot in Hades where the cattle come from."

"Maybe not, Henry, but I don't want us to get reckless."

"Reckon you're right," admitted the hardcase. "But we will make a raid against the N Bar—which'll pleasure me considerable." His guttural laughter pushed away with the gentle breeze.

Twisting in the saddle, Black Jack made a come-up-here sign to his brother Will and Jess Williams. "You boys fork on ahead and find us a saloon which ain't too crowded." And the other outlaws broke their horses away, setting them into a hard ground-eating canter, for they'd been out of any hard stuff for the last week and had money to burn. And watching them go, their leader knew they'd behave themselves and not cause any undo ruckus. All of them were wary that way, to go into a place quietly and mingle with the locals and treat for a round or two. He knew that friend of Long Henry's, Sixtoes Baker, would behave. But it was Henry himself he had to worry about. The man was a keg of dynamite about to explode, and he hoped it wouldn't happen in Box Elder. If it did, he might have no other choice than to get rid of Thompson.

When they were about a couple of hundred yards out, they

pulled toward the creek and rode through the screening brush
to dismount along the south bank. From here they'd pair up
and go in, with Bob Hays and George Musgrove now pulling
away toward the main trail. A bunch of riders entering any
small cowtown drew attention. In a little while two more departed, the last to leave Black Jack and Sixtoes Baker. In time
they, too, rode into Box Elder, cloaked in the darker fabric of
night, and easily found the horses of the others tied up in front
and around a side wall of a log cabin saloon that occupied a
lonely place on the northern outskirts of town.

"Place I'd pick," Baker said idly, as he tied up his reins. He
was in a good mood now that they were here. He'd come to
like Black Jack's company, along with admiring the way the
man was ramrodding things. Now he couldn't help smiling at
the full moon low to the east. "I knew this doctor, down in
Wichita, tellin' me a lot of strange things happen where there's
a full moon. Causes ordinary folks to do weird things . . .
killin' . . . women gettin' bitchier'n all get-out."

Turning to gaze that way, a frown lined Black Jack's forehead. *All we need is to have somethin' happen. Just hope it
doesn't make Long Henry pop his cork* . . . His eyes swung
to a man staggering out of the saloon, from his ragged clothing
a down-and-outer. Farther toward town he looked over the tidy
homes throwing out light and the two streets heading toward
the saloon. It seemed homey enough, but this was a place
where violence often happened with a killing swiftness. *Let
me and the boys just get drunk in peace.*

On a street in the center of Box Elder, town marshal Parker
Dillingham was working his teeth over with a toothpick as he
stood in front of a cafe, his belly full and feeling awfully con-
tented. Though one of the waitresses had made a snide com-
ment as he left about his being a big fat hog. If he was up to
it, he'd have thrown back some retort. But what the hell, there
was always tomorrow to get his licks in.

He muttered, "Anyway, opinions are like assholes: everyone's got one."

One thing about Dillingham was that he knew he wasn't much of a lawman, but he had his pride. When fights broke out, he made it a habit to show up later when things got calmed down. And there was this stock detective, Dunn, pulling in, which he resented somewhat, since Parker Dillingham had never drawn down on anyone. Just a little while ago he'd seen Dunn entering the Carbine Hotel, and he snorted, "Vivian is sure sweet on that . . . hero."

Rolling the toothpick around in his mouth, he patted his stomach with both hands and set out to try and cadge a drink or two at one of the saloons. And as he did, Dillingham took in the lone horseman swinging down in front of Murdock's livery stable. The stranger had on one of those tan Hudson Bay coats, and was kind of dark-skinned. The marshal went on by, drawn by his need for some hard liquor and maybe a game of cards.

The man was Pierre LaFleur, his gaze moving from the passing fat man to the hostler coming out holding a hay fork. Without too much ado, he left his horse in care of the hostler and, before leaving, got the location of the few saloons. Upon riding in, he'd spotted the horses belonging to the High Fives tethered around the log cabin saloon, this fact telling him the outlaws hadn't as yet secured lodging for the night. As he was about to do. He was a practical man, taking care of the little things first, for the little overlooked things could come back later to haunt you.

He went downstreet and got a room at the Carbine Hotel, then went up to his room and refreshened himself. Then LaFleur enjoyed a leisurely supper in the dining room, where he caught a glimpse of an attractive woman leaving with a man wearing a badge. His quiet inquiries of the waitress revealed that the man was stock inspector Nick Dunn.

So this is the lawman Glendenning has in his back pocket. As yet, Pierre LaFleur hadn't heard about how Dunn had taken out the Red Miller gang. That Dunn was in town, though, could mean trouble if the High Fives decided they were offended by the man's badge. As for the town marshal of this hayseed town, he'd been informed by the waitress that the man was no threat to anyone. All LaFleur wanted was for this night to pass uneventfully, and then for the High Fives to vamoose.

On the ride down, he knew it was a big risk if they followed Ralph Glendenning's wishes and hit the N Bar N ranch. He would have to talk this over with Black Jack Christian. At his nod, the waitress refilled his coffee cup as he said pleasantly, "Now, what do we have for dessert?"

Meanwhile, the men he had come to see were making themselves comfortable at Bilken's Log Cabin saloon. Every window was open to the warm night, as were the doors. They had ingratiated themselves with the townspeople, just a handful that had trickled in, the bar being presided over by Millie DeRod, a middle-aged woman smoking a cigarillo as she sat at a table with Will Christian and Three-Fingered Jack Dunlop. She ran the place for her husband, who'd been crippled in a hunting accident, these strangers chancing in a sudden windfall. She caught the eye of one of her bartenders and said, "Another round over here, Burt. So, Will, we're pretty much isolated from the mainstream of life. Just a waystop on the main line between Great Falls and Havre; if you can call those burgs big cities, which I can't. Boys, someday I want to walk down Park Avenue and waltz right into a fancy New York hotel. Now there's a city."

"I was in Rio once," volunteered Dunlop. "My pa was a seaman in the merchant marines . . . and my brothers got into that, too. Just didn't like gettin' seasick every time I was on one of those ships. Even before we pulled anchor I could feel it comin' on."

Will Christian cleared his throat, and he was about to say something, only to hold back and stare at the sudden onslaught of angry voices coming from the table occupied by Long Henry Thompson. He watched as Black Jack pushed up to go over and settle the matter between Thompson, who had been really putting away the liquor, and a townsman. Now Will's attention was drawn to the front door and the arrival of town marshal Dillingham wedging his obese frame through and smiling his way to the bar. Wonder flared in Will Christian's eyes when he noticed the badge pinned to the fat man's vest, and he said to Millie DeRod, "Bet that gent weighs three hundred pounds, or more."

"Parker, yeah, our illustrious town marshal. Harmless as a dry fart on a windy day. That sixgun he's packing, don't think it's ever been cleaned. Hey, Parker, get your fat ass over here." She smiled at her table companions.

Waddling over, and all smiles as he did, he said, "Why, Millie, does this mean we're engaged . . ."

"No, but plant your ass on that chair and I'll spring for a drink or two." She threw the names of her table companions at the marshal, who was all too pleased just to be part of a drinking crowd where maybe he didn't have to buy any drinks, judging from the money spilled carelessly before the pair of strangers. His pleasure increased immeasurably when a bartender came up and shoved a glass of beer before him.

Of a different mood was Black Jack Christian, now seated at a table with Buck "Sixtoes" Baker. As far as the locals knew, they were just a couple of strangers stopping for a drink before passing on through. He hadn't so much as thrown a glance at the other members of his gang, other than unobtrusively settling the argument between Thompson and another patron though his wary eyes had checked out everything of importance in this barroom. He liked Baker in that the man could carry on an intelligent conversation, and do it quietly. He was picking up little tidbits of information from those seated at nearby tables, most of it about this rustling epidemic.

"LaFleur—he's late."

He nodded at Baker and said, "We've got all night, Buck."

"Think I'll mosey over to that side table an' help myself to some more of that venison sausage and that bean soup. You want some?"

"Well," Black Jack said, "he just walked in."

Sixtoes Baker sank down onto his chair as Pierre LaFleur checked out the room before sauntering toward the tables.

There were two empty chairs, and LaFleur chose the one giving him a view of the front door. He was all smiles, but even so he didn't say much until he'd looked around to locate the other hardcases. Briefly, he gazed at the town marshal jawing away, dismissing the man as merely a nuisance wearing a badge. "So, my friends, it is good that you are all looking well."

"How's your lawyer friend—"

"Owly, as usual. He wants someone killed."

Interest flickered in Black Jack's eyes.

"Tom Wilson is foreman out at the N Bar N ranch."

"I know that place," said Baker. "But . . . doesn't this lawyer have somethin' to do with the N Bar?"

"Whatever." LaFleur shrugged. "I know our plans were for you to take your men way west, Black Jack. What do you think about raiding the N Bar? After all, the man who kills this Wilson earns an extra five hundred . . ."

"There was a time when I'd kill a man for a double eagle and change. What do you think, Pierre, that just perhaps Glendenning is runnin' scared . . ."

"Exactly." The Canuck smiled. "The question now is, my friends, do we need him anymore. We are the risk takers, not the illustrious lawyer."

"Be a lot more money for me and my boys. So, Pierre, I'll let you get rid of Glendenning. I don't trust lawyers. Meanin' that we just can't let him keep stewin' up there in Havre once he learns we've cut him out. He could sic the law on us."

"Tres bien, I shall give our benefactor the *aborrecimiento* of death before using my knife. Now on to more important things." He hunkered in closer to Black Jack as Sixtoes Baker pushed up and headed over to the side table to get some grub. LaFleur began detailing just where he would be waiting to take the cattle off Black Jack's hands.

Engrossed in their conversation, their eyes merely brushed

past the couple entering the barroom. Nick Dunn wasn't at all sure about bringing Vivian in here. Yet any objections he was about to utter were left unsaid when the owner of the saloon, Millie DeRod, came over to them. "Vivian, been a while. And who is this handsome gent?"

Before Vivian could respond, the whiskey-slurred voice of Long Henry Thompson cut through the pale light in the barroom, "Dunn, you back-shootin' scum . . . I knew I'd run into you . . ." As he rose, Thompson's chair spilled over backward, the man staring bullets at Nick Dunn, and all around him chairs were quickly vacated.

The shock of this abating, Nick gestured for the women to move toward the bar. It suddenly occurred to him that he was probably the only person in here who knew Long Henry. Out of the corner of his eye he spotted town marshal Dillingham hunkered low in his chair, and Nick said loudly, "Marshal, the loudmouth yonder is wanted for murder. He's Long Henry Thompson . . . and I—"

"Leave that bag of hoss manure out of it, Dunn! This is between me and you. So you're a big-shot stock inspector now. But the way you wear your gun tells me you're somethin' else . . . maybe a high liner like me . . ."

"Enough Thompson," snarled Nick Dunn. "Unbuckle your gunbelt as I'm arres—" Then he saw his antagonist's hand blurring toward his gun, and Nick reached for his own. His Colt was just clearing leather when a slug from Long Henry's sixgun struck him solidly, and he fired back almost wildly. He knew he'd hit Thompson; then he was hit again, to his disbelief, things began getting fuzzy, and his legs, though he wasn't aware of it, were buckling. He half-turned to face Vivian staring ashen-faced back at him, and he started to apologize for all of this; but instead he pitched forward and was dead before his body hit the sawdust-covered floorboards.

"It was a fair fight," yelled Long Henry. He ignored the bullet wound to his left forearm, perhaps not even realizing that he'd been hit, turning some to get most of the patrons into the limits of his vision.

"What about it, Parker," someone said loudly, "you're the law here in Box Elder."

"I . . . I . . . yeah, I seen it all." He lumbered to his feet, not certain if the tall stranger would turn that gun on him, scared so bad he could barely stand. "Go . . . go about your business, everybody. I . . . I'll go fetch the coroner." He stumbled past Vivian McCauley, who had knelt down by Nick Dunn's body, and damn near took the batwings with him in his flight out of the saloon.

Now someone had the common sense to come over and place his coat over Nick Dunn's face, as he said gently to Vivian, "Ma'am, he's dead . . . and there's nothin' we can do about that." He gestured, and Mille DeRod came over and placed a comforting arm around Vivian's shoulder, urging the weeping woman away from the body and out onto the front porch.

"Isn't . . . isn't anybody going to arrest that man?"

"For sure not our cowardly town marshal."

"But he's that outlaw, Henry Thompson?"

"Come now, Viv, honey, my house is just up the street. Something'll be done, I'm sure. Come now, honey."

TWELVE

The morning stage brought Tom Wilson back into Box Elder, and as it rolled to a halt on Main Street, one of those idling under the shading porch of the stagecoach office blurted out, "You boys should have been here last night. There was a shoot-out over at Millie's place between Nick Dunn and Long Henry Thompson. Dunn got killed and Thompson vamoosed."

"The hell you say?"

"I was there when it happened," the man added, though he hadn't been, and just by saying this he hoped to secure a place in western legend. He rambled on some more as Tom Wilson moved away.

Tom mused, *A terrible thing to happen to anybody. But how is Vivian taking all of this? As she'd been sweet on Nick. I reckon he tried to arrest Long Henry.* Strong to Tom came scenes of what had happened during spring roundup. Of how the drunken Henry Thompson had so callously murdered his cook, the role that Dunn had played, that somehow this was the way of it sometimes. Kismet, or whatever. His first intentions were of taking the money Glendenning had so reluctantly given him over to the bank to square the N Bar account. But that could wait until he had gone to see Vivian McCauley.

Coming off the boardwalk and striding across an intersection, he saw town marshal Parker Dillingham emerging from his office, and Tom called out, "Hold up, Parker." He went on to step onto the planking as Dillingham muttered, "I expect you want to talk to me about the killing, Tom. It happened so suddenlike a man didn't have time to think . . . or realize what was goin' on."

Sharply Tom said, "Why haven't you formed a posse?"

"Tried to, Tom," he said evasively. "S'matter of fact, some of those who'd been over at Millie's did take off after Long Henry."

"Any men I know?"

"Well, Goldstein, the jeweler, and Daggett, and some strangers that chanced to be there. Sure, Tom, they cut out after Long Henry just after I returned with the coroner." He added lamely, "You know, Tom, I don't fit on a horse too well . . ."

In softer tones Tom said, "I reckon so. Yeah, Dunn was a stock inspector . . . and I suppose you did fire off a wire to W.D. Smith about this . . ."

His eyes brightening, Dillingham said, "Why, Tom, I was just on my way over to the telegraph office. I'll . . . I'll see you later . . ." It had never occurred to him to do this, and he blundered away at the reprieve just handed him by Tom Wilson.

Watching the man go, Tom could only shake his head. Never in his wildest imaginings, he reckoned, did poor ol' Parker ever think something of this nature would happen. It wasn't that Parker was a coward, just a man of limited vision, the type you saw in darn near every cowtown. They ran with the pack, only sometimes, like now in Parker Dillingham's case, the pack would be eyeing him, since as town marshal he was now the town's alpha wolf. And the truth of it all was that Parker didn't know how to handle the situation. "So, I've known some incompetent lawyers, too."

Going on to enter the lobby of the Carbine Hotel, he was told that Vivian McCauley was up in her rooms. He knew the way, and soon was rapping gently on her door. He removed his Stetson and knocked again, and this time it opened slightly. Vivian's face was drawn, the lines showing plainly as she didn't have on any makeup. She managed a smile for Tom as he entered the living room of her three-room suite. "Tom, how nice of you to drop up."

"I just heard about it," he said.

"Don't misunderstand, Nick was just a friend. We went over to Millie's to have a drink. Tom, it just happened . . . mere chance, I suppose, this outlaw being there. The next thing I knew they'd drawn on one another. And . . . Nick was killed . . ."

"While he worked for me," said Tom, "Nick Dunn never hesitated to take on the dirty jobs. I expect the stockman's association will foot the cost of the funeral."

"Yes, I suppose they will. Did things work out up in Havre?"

"Had to really work to get the money out of that lawyer. Vivian, I guess I'd better go, as I've got some chores to tend to."

"Then you'll be leaving for the ranch. Right now I've half a mind to get out of Box Elder." Her eyes followed him to the door. "And again, Mr. Wilson, thanks for coming up."

At that very moment, the photographer who'd taken those pictures of stock detective Nick Dunn was trying to peddle copies of them at one of the saloons. He'd sold three pictures at a dollar apiece, and had cornered blacksmith Phil Larkin, who seemed interested but just then had spent his last bit of pocket change on a stein of beer. "Sure, mister, I'd like to buy one of those pictures. Say two of 'em in exchange for shoein' your hoss?"

One of the pictures had been stuck up behind the bar, and the photographer said proudly, "Someday that picture'll be as famous as that one of the Wild Bunch. Sure, my horse needs some new iron under its hoofs. Now, is there anybody else in here wanting to acquire one of these historical artifacts showing the famous Nick Dunn and three local favorites. Remember, folks, Mr. Dunn single-handedly took out the Red Miller gang. You sir, one picture, that'll be a silver dollar."

Someone rushed into the room to yell that the posse was returning, and the saloon emptied out into the street. But instead of several riders and perhaps the killer Long Henry

Thompson roped over his saddle, there were only three men astride tired horses.

"Well, where are the others?"

"Still keeping after Thompson, I guess," said jeweler Morris Goldstein. With some effort he swung down. "As far as we could gather, Long Henry headed for the Missouri Breaks. Now if you'll excuse me, I have to open for business."

But instead of heading for their hideout in the breaks, the High Fives had in fact caught up to gunslinger Henry Thompson. They were settled in by a creek, where Will Christian was checking out the bullet wound to Thompson's forearm. He didn't reckon it was anything serious, as it seemed the bullet had just cut through flesh and missed any bones. After sterilizing the wound with whiskey, he wrapped a torn piece of cloth around Thompson's arm, the man sober now and trying to rid himself of a headache by throwing down coffee.

Black Jack had just returned with an armload of firewood. He dropped it down by the campfire and brushed debris from his clothing as he regarded through debating eyes the one weak link, he figured now, in this rustling setup. Nodding his thanks at the cup handed him by Jess Williams, he came in to hunker down by Thompson. "Henry," he said quietly, "that was a stupid play. No . . . I don't want any of your lip. Now you hear me out, Henry. If I cut you loose right now, you know you won't last long, as every lawman in Montana is looking to find you. Your problem is you just can't seem to control your temper, an' next thing'll happen we're someplace drinkin' you'll take it out on someone else. Only this time we won't be so lucky."

"So I drink." He scowled.

Black Jack let this go as he sipped from his cup. Then he said, but deeper and with an ugly tint in his voice, "By rights I should plug you and leave you here for the turkey vultures. But I won't, as you've done your share of the hard work and taken the risks, same's us, Henry. Now I want you to think

about all of this hard, dammit. As you've come to the end of
your rope with me an' the High Fives."

"I have pushed it," he admitted. "Just when these dark
moods take hold'a me, Black Jack, well, I get hotter'n a cornbread fart."

"Good, an' I've got some good news for you, Henry. And
you others, gather around." He took the time to shape a tailor-made as everyone moved closer to the camp fire. "First of
all, we won't, at least for now, be makin' the long ride over
to the Rockies. LaFleur wants us to hit the N Bar N ranch.
The big thing is he's put a bounty on the head of Tom Wilson,
the N Bar foreman. You said you worked there, Henry . . ."

"Yup, and I know the layout cold. As for Wilson, I 'spect
we'll find him at the home buildings. About two hours shy of
sundown right now. We leave soon, we'll pull in there, oh,
around eleven tonight. When things are nice and quiet." He
forgot about his headache and the ache coming from his forearm, allowing a smile to split his lips. "Then after we take
out Wilson, it's a simple matter of heading due northwest
where the bigger herd is grazing."

"What about your arm?"

"What about that bounty?" countered Long Henry.

"Five hundred to the man downin' Tom Wilson."

"My arm feels a helluva lot better. Sixtoes, pass over one
of them stogies."

Once he got a glimpse of the Teton River, Henry Thompson
knew they were on N Bar ranch land. He was headman of the
rustlers tonight, had led them past some cowhands guarding a
scattered bunch of cattle, ever angling to the northwest while
guiding by the North Star.

Under starlight, a stiff wind casting away the sound of their
horses, they rode on. If they rested, it was briefly, for in all
of them was this sense of expectancy, like when a man knew
the card just dealt him would fill a royal flush. Soon Long

Henry's arm went up, pointing toward a lonely butte he'd ridden by many a time before.

Slowing to a walk, he said tautly, "Half a mile to the home buildings."

"Somebody's sure to still be up," said Black Jack.

"Yeah, Black Jack, folks stay up late around here in the summertime. How's it to be?"

He smiled around his words, "You're callin' it."

"So then you take your brother and Hays and Musgrove. An' you cut around west of the bluff. Beyond that you'll be on higher ground, so you should pick up on the rest of us beelinin' right on in. You can't miss that big mangy piece of house. The bunkhouse is between that and the big barn."

"Pull your bandannas over your faces," cautioned Black Jack. "We just goin' for Tom Wilson, or what?"

"Wilson's mine," spat out Thompson. "There might be a couple of hands over there and a cook. I figure we just take out Wilson and hightail it. Or, Black Jack, it's your call—"

"Whatever. Just that we won't hang around. We still have to get at that herd and push it along damned fast." He spurred away, followed by some of the rustlers.

Long Henry Thompson took the direct route east of the butte and was soon coming in on an outer corral that wasn't used much anymore. The buildings looked forlorn and deserted, until Three-Fingered Jack pointed out window light glowing from the bunkhouse. Farther along, and once they had passed the barn, Thompson said, "There's a light on in the main house; seems to be comin' from the kitchen. As I recall, Wilson would get a late snack before hittin' the sack. We'll try that first."

He brought the rustlers almost silently along the south wall of the house and just short of the back wall, where Thompson swung down and handed his reins to Sixtoes Baker. Gruffly he said, "This is a job for one man. But keep your eyes peeled to that bunkhouse."

Grasping his Colt .45, Thompson went boldly around to the back and stood there gazing through a kitchen window. He could see reflected movement, and that was enough for him, as he simply opened the screen door and strode into the kitchen. There was a man in the kitchen. It wasn't the person he sought, but the cook, and he thumbed the hammer back and demanded, "Wilson, where is he?"

"Gone . . . gone to Box Elder . . ." He could barely stand in the fear of what was happening, though he'd raised his arms over his head.

"Damn," the outlaw cursed. Letting his anger subside, he knew that a shot would roust the hands in the bunkhouse. He was hot to kill, though, and he took a giant stride forward and simply swept his gun barrel across the man's face. The cook slammed back into a counter and from there dropped limply to the floor. Reaching for the butcher knife the man had been using to cut a slab of cured ham, he leaned and sank the blade as deep as he could into the unconscious man's stomach and simply left the knife there. Now he rummaged about until he found a gunnysack, which he filled with two hunks of ham and other foodstuffs.

Pushing outside, he went around to tie the gunnysack to his saddle as he said, "Wilson's gone. We'll pull out quietly." When he was mounted, he led them to higher ground, where they soon ran into the others.

Thompson explained the situation to Black Jack, who said after due consideration, "Yup, at least we got some grub. Could be come morning when they find that cook, it'll appear to the others he just might have committed suicide."

"Now listen up," cut in Thompson. "Five miles north of here is where they're holding the main herd. As it's the best grazing land on this ranch. We don't know how many men will be standin' guard duty, which could be a problem."

"Naw," jeered Jess Williams, "nothin' we can't handle."

And they rode out, but slowly as to keep the sound of their horses from revealing their presence to the men still back at the home buildings. In him as he rode was a sense of unease, but instead of pushing it away, Black Jack Christian tried to locate its source. Maybe it was that flippant remark of Jess's that had brought this on. Or even now someone could be headin' for the kitchen in hopes of some food. Then there was the cattle they were about to steal; tonight they would have to get in and out quickly. *In the past we've always lurked about to check out everything. Can't do that now with that dead man back there. Should we just pull out of here and leave these cattle alone?* No, the die was cast about that. And if he did, his men would damn well question his leadership role.

The route taken by Tom Wilson on his way back to the N Bar was more direct than the one that had gotten him to Box Elder. To tell the truth, he was in a hurry to get back. Though it helped to know the country, a long time after nightfall he was finally forced to jog the stallion down along a stream, where he let it drink. After he tied up the horse, he removed the saddle and saddlebags and his bedroll and arranged them where he was going to sleep. Then he got a fire going, a small one, barely enough to heat some coffee.

As he sat drinking from his tin cup, and nibbling on some crackers, he thought back to his reappearance at the bank in Box Elder. Once he'd deposited the money to the N Bar account, he drafted a letter with the help of Otto Vetter, who'd promised to mail it on to the absentee owners. This was the first step, Tom figured, in a fight between him and Glendenning over just who was to run the ranch. At least these owners were businessmen, and would take the wiser course.

Nick Dunn dead and gone—among others. Before pulling out of Box Elder, he'd gone back to the Carbine Hotel for something to eat, and his hopes were answered, too, when he found Vivian in the dining room. This time when they talked it was with the realization on her part that nothing could be changed about Dunn. Again she had told him quite bluntly that they'd only been friends. A man knew when a woman liked him or wanted him around; at least this was the impression Vivian had left with him as he'd departed to get the stallion and leave town.

He poured the remaining coffee into his cup and set the pot down by the dying embers of the fire. With the cup in hand he moved over and arranged his bedroll, and then sat down to brace his back against his saddle and, as he always did when camped out, turn his eyes to study the sky. Like most cattlemen this was the last thing they did before hitting their bedrolls. To his relief the sky was startlingly clear as he'd ever seen it, and with no moonlight to diffuse the glow of the stars. The Milky Way looked invitingly close, and he smiled inwardly, recalling the sage words of a preacher on this.

As I recollect, they went somethin' like this. In that many folks, men and women, are always searching for somethin' better, never satisfied, always seeking to find a place where the grass is greener. That the truth is it never gets better, that what you see or have and hold is the best of it for a lot of people. Like tonight . . . this land and this sky . . . and the good Lord a 'lookin' down. Man don't appreciate this, he should pack it in.

"And, too, how are things back on the ranch?" Tom said, as his stallion whickered softly in response.

Constantly his mind would go to how his men were faring, and the cattle, all because of the rustling activity. To this end, he had gotten all of his hands together and spilled out a plan he'd devised. For some it would be like standing sentinel duty much like a soldier, but if it saved their lives, Tom figured that was all that mattered. Fortunately his men were experienced cowhands, every one of them fairly proficient with firearms. Would rustlers hit at the N Bar?

"Not if but when." Now Tom snuggled under his bedroll and tipped his hat low over his forehead and tried to shut everything away. One of his last thoughts was of rising early, maybe around four, to finish the two-day trip. Then he began dozing away.

And as sleep finally came to Tom Wilson, about twenty miles away the voice of an N Bar hand rose in an old standard of a western song to drift over the dark mass of cattle already settled in for the night. Les Aston didn't mind ridin' nighthawk guard all that much, though he wished he could use his guitar to accompany his voice. He was one of five riders scattered about the cattle taking up around a half-mile circle. Some would go clockwise, the rest the other way, and they'd encounter one another to exchange small talk, which mostly was about rustling. None of them wanted to be simply slaughtered like those Circle W hands had been.

Farther out more N Bar cowhands held to higher ground, ten of them and in pairs, with their horses tethered nearby and saddled. One of them was Clemet Hall, whose eyes had gone sleepy, but sleep was a chore being undertaken by the other waddy with him, Sid Osborne. It had taken some time to get used to this nightly chore of holding out here, for them a ledge along the side of a low-slung butte. But from it they could see for miles, to better enable them to detect night riders coming in.

Hearing Osborne stirring awake, he said to the waddy, "Awful tough sleepin' on this rock pile."

"Yup. What time is it?"

"Dunno—two, two-thirty. You've got a watch, so you tell me."

"If the blamed thing works." Sid Osborne fumbled for his watch and a sulphur, which he struck into flame against his belt buckle. "Almost three, Clemet. I might as well keep watch and let you have a go at sleepin' until first light." He jabbed the wooden match into the loamy ground to douse the flame. All he had to do was adjust his hat, which he did now, to be fully clothed, and somewhat wearily he got up to move over and squat down next to Hall.

"Lot of cattle down there."

"Nearly five thousand."

"Smaller bunches scattered about. You see that?"

"Where about, Sid?"

"Could be some deer, like that bunch we spotted last night. Southwest of here . . . by that long red patch of elevation."

"Still can't make nothin' out . . ."

"Movin' north of that now . . . maybe two miles from the herd."

"Okay, now I've got whatever it is located. No moon; could be anything."

Sid Osborne's loud whistle thrilled away to the north, and he had to whistle again before an answering whistle came back. Then he called out loudly, "Ridley, we might have company. Train that field glass of yours to about a mile or two south of the herd . . . between that treeline and those breaks."

A hundred yards away waddy Josh Ridley soon got the field glass pressed to his right eye. It took some time for him to focus in on the area in question, simply because of the deeper blackness clinging to the land. But when he did, he caught shadowy movement of animals pressing along quickly toward the herd ground. Through the uncertainties pounding at him, came a sudden fear, an instant recalling of storys told and retold around camp fires of the atrocities committed by these rustlers. Until you were a part of it, perhaps now, it all seemed dreamlike. Now he caught the shape of a rider astride a horse, more of them, and he yelled back at Osborne and Hall, "I make out about ten of them . . . heading fast for the herd."

That was all Clemet Hall needed to hear as he brought up his Winchester and began peppering bullets into the night sky. And as he did, Sid Osborne was scrambling for their horses. Hall realized this might stampede the cattle, but there was no way out of it, for the reverberating roar of his rifle, he knew, had punched into the ears of his friends down with the herd. Then he was by his horse and jamming the Winchester back into the boot and claiming his saddle. Like the ten other waddies holding to high places, he was reining hard to get to the herd ground.

Down on the level plain, Les Aston knew instantly what was happening, and he drew his sixgun and spun his horse around as his searching eyes sought out the raiders. To the south, a gun sounded, and just like that the mass of cattle was in motion, a tidal wave of black rippling away to the north and scattering out as they stampeded. This was what Tom Wilson had drummed into them, to let the cattle go and try to take out the rustlers.

Much to his relief he encountered another hand, and they exchanged excited questions, and then Aston barked, "South of us, Bill. A bunch headin' this way . . . so let's get the thievin' son'bitches . . ." Together they rode, firing their weapons to create more confusion for the raiders.

And Black Jack knew they had lost control of the situation when he heard one of his men scream out in pain and then flop out of the saddle. Then another rustler went down, as they now found themselves returning fire, it seemed, from men sweeping in from all directions. Through this, Long Henry was cursing away and firing randomly.

Black Jack yelled out, "What the hell, let's make tracks out of here! Will . . . where are you . . . Will Christian, answer me!" Just to his left another man took a hit and nose-dived to the ground, his horse galloping on after the other rustlers led now by Sixtoes Baker.

Somehow Black Jack got his horse into motion, gripped by the uncertainties of what had happened to his brother, damning in his mind the stupidity of this raid against the N Bar ranch. He screamed out as a bullet tugged at his hat, "All because that lawyer is runnin' scared. If Will's gone down, Glendenning, you're a dead man."

Realizing the rustlers were backtracking to get away, the N Bar hands swung in after them for about a mile, until Les Aston, who'd been placed in charge by his foreman, yelled for them to give up the chase. They reined up in dusty confusion, strung out to either side in a ragged line, and then they began coming together, still scared and awed that they were still alive. Their voices mingled together as each man had something to say, but calmer now, the sound of the horses ridden by the raiders dimming away into the night.

"The cattle are scattered from here to Canada," someone said.

Gruffly Les Aston said, "I want a head count. So spout out your name." Worriedly he listened to their responses, and then he said, "Osborne, what about him?"

Clemet Hall said, "We was together comin' in on the herd, Les. Then some cattle got in to split us up. Come on, let's check it out."

The concerned men broke back to the north, spreading out by order of Aston. Their search reached a sudden halt when coming toward them at a limp and leading his horse was the missing waddy, who said, "Some loco steer came hookin' in and almost gored me where it counts."

"How bad you hurt, Sid?"

"Tore some flesh, is about all, I reckon."

"Okay, Sid, you go to the main camp and get a fire going. The rest of us'll set out after the cattle." He squinted northerly at a riderless horse holding as if it had no place to go. He still held his sixgun, and now he thumbed the hammer back. Grimly he added, "Some of them went down. Come on, we'll check it out. But slow and cautious easy."

It took less than five minutes for them to locate the bodies of three dead rustlers, and Aston got down to make sure. Straightening up, he said, "Now they're good rustlers. Okay, let's track out after the cattle."

Other men were on the prowl tonight.

They were the hunters, just the two of them, but unlike the High Fives, these men were on the side of the law. So far the big game they were after had eluded them. But they were closing in, a thought that had kept U.S. Marshal Harlow Bennett and Mountie Doug McCray pressing on.

A day ago they had been in Box Elder, where they'd learned about the killing of that stock detective. They'd seen no reason to identify themselves as they prowled about getting the facts, and soon were tagging after the posse. It wasn't long before they had run into three riders, to learn these men had been part of the posse and were on their way back to Box Elder. Out of this both Bennett and Mountie McCray had come to the realization that the men keeping after Long Henry Thompson were actually his outlaw friends.

Back a distance they had come across a creek where their quarry had made camp. Heat still came from the dying fire, so they knew they were closing in, the tracks they honed in on going straight to the northwest as if these men knew where they were going. Sorting this out as the day ended, Marshal Bennett determined the outlaws were going to hit the N Bar N ranch.

They rode along boldly, knowing the outlaws, if they did stop to camp, would avail themselves of a campfire. He said to McCray, "Maybe we should have taken off after N Bar foreman Tom Wilson. After all, he was up in Havre holding a powwow with this lawyer. I know this is all mixed together somehow, Doug."

"Pierre LaFleur has to be parded up with these men, too."

"This makes two men that Thompson has gunned down. We know he came into Box Elder with a lot of money to spend. I figure the whole rustling gang was there. But from the descriptions given us, they're strangers to these parts. Up ahead now, Doug, is that butte guarding the home buildings. Seems to be a light on in one of the buildings."

Closing in, they soon could discern more clearly the outlines of the buildings, to find the light was coming from around the back of a big house. They rode in warily, needing to take a breather and hoping to get some coffee or something warm to eat. Bennett reached to touch McCray's arm, and he said softly, "Yonder's the bunkhouse; but let's check out the house first."

They walked their horses toward where light was still pouring out of the kitchen. By the worn path drifting away from the back door they dismounted, with McCray holding the reins as his comrade took a quick glance in a kitchen window. Now

Bennett moved over and rapped on the screen door, and receiving no response, he opened the door and entered the kitchen.

Right away he set his grimacing eyes upon the butcher knife protruding from the stomach of the man lying on the floor. "Those bastards beat us here," he said angrily. He turned and shoved through an inner door and called out loudly, "Anybody here!" Through the silence enveloping him he had the feeling the house was empty. He spun around and returned to the back screen door, and narrated to McCray what he had found in the kitchen.

McCray said ominously, "I hate to think of what we'll find in the bunkhouse."

"Let's find out," Bennett said, as he wrapped a big hand around the butt of his sixgun and unleathered it, whereupon he triggered the weapon into the air. The rippling sound had barely died away when someone yelled out a bunkhouse window, "That you, Fred, firing at a coyote again?"

"You, in the bunkhouse, this is U.S. Marshal Harlow Bennett! I've tracked some rustlers thisaway."

"The hell you say, Marshal," a cowhand yelled back skeptically.

"I say they've been here . . . 'cause we just found a man stabbed to death in the kitchen. Me and Mountie McCray will hold out here in the light so you'll know this is no ambush."

In a matter of moments the three cowpunchers that had been occupying the bunkhouse came in out of the darkness from different directions, holding sixguns and one of them a rifle. One man exclaimed, "Yeah, he's Bennett all right, as I seen him in Havre one time. You say you tracked some rustlers over here?"

"Among them will be Henry Thompson. It could have been Thompson takin' that butcher knife to your cook. Who's ramroddin' this outfit now?"

"Tom Wilson; but he went to Box Elder," the cowboy threw back as he crowded behind the other hands pushing into the kitchen, with Bennett and McCray coming in behind. Through stony faces everyone stared down at the dead man.

Until one of the hands commented, "They must have snuck in here damned quietlike. Wonder why they didn't come after us?"

"Strange that they came here in the first place," questioned McCray.

"More importantly," said Marshal Bennett, "is where are they going tonight. I figure to rustle some N Bar cattle."

"The main herd is being grazed north of here about half a dozen miles. Reckon we'd better saddle our hosses and head up there, Marshal. Just hope we're not too late."

"Well," said another hand, "if them rustlers do try anything, they're in for a big surprise. I'll explain on the way, Marshal." Then he trooped after the others hurrying outside to head for a corral at a run.

As the screen door slammed shut, Marshal Bennett saw no reason not to help himself to some coffee, as did McCray. But before drinking any coffee, he reached for a big towel and placed it over the dead man's upper body. When he straightened up, anger glittered in his eyes over this senseless killing act. McCray found a loaf of bread in a cupboard and some bacon that had been fried. He fashioned a couple of sandwiches and handed one to Bennett, then said, "I was going to enter the priesthood, Harlow. Away back when I had some common sense left."

"Nobody in his right mind ever becomes a lawman," agreed Bennett. "It's going on three by my watch. Soon the sun'll be comin' up. Another sleepless night for the pair of us. Only wish we had been here sooner."

Then a cowhand whistled shrilly from where he sat his bronc behind the house, and the lawmen strode outside chomping on sandwiches as they reclaimed their saddles. The cowhand took the point at a chippy canter, but once they were clear of the buildings, the gait picked up considerably.

THIRTEEN

Tom Wilson pushed along as false dawn crept palely into the sky. He'd been in the saddle for nearly an hour, and he wasn't following any discernible trail, the stallion as eager as he was to get onto home range. Coming through some sagebrush, he heard the whirring wings of a night hawk diving on some prey. Along the way he had encountered other night hunters, cattle, and deer which were out grazing away from the thick brush and timber they liked to hide among during the day.

Chimney rock on a butte ahead told him he was right on course, and that in about another fifteen minutes he should be running into some N Bar cattle. Once he had cleared the butte, instead of reining to the south, Tom kept heading due west. *The main herd . . . it won't do any harm to check it out. Anyway, buy the time I get there they'll have mornin' coffee brewing.*

This was mostly open prairie interspaced with elevations, about the best grazing land to be found anywhere. There were gorging rivers and smaller streams and wetlands, where waterfowl hung out. A man, he knew, couldn't ask for more than this. He didn't mind being a ranch foreman, though he would like to latch on to a small spread, and he knew he could make a go of it. But not alone, his thoughts returning to Box Elder and Vivian McCauley. *Make a man a good wife.*

He wasn't sure at first, as it wasn't all that light yet; then he heard a shrill "yippeee," and some cattle came busting out of a draw followed by a cowpuncher. He wasn't sure if it was one of his hands or not, and was uncertain about riding on to intercept the man. As the rider became outlined, the shape of the man's hat told him it was Clemet Hall, and Tom whistled shrilly as he whipped off his hat and waved it over his head.

He went on only after Hall had thrown back a come-on wave. Spurring on at a canter, he soon joined up with the waddie, who said, "Dammit, Tom, you should'a been here last night. We got hit, by them damned rustlers."

"Anybody get hurt?"

"Nope, as we was plumb lucky about that. It was your idea, Tom, of putting out guards that turned the trick in our favor." Clemet Hall grinned wickedly. "We got three of the bastards, too."

"I reckon they stampeded the herd."

"Scattered 'em all over the range. But, heck, won't be no time a'tall before we got the herd back together. How many were there? Not all that many . . . less'n a dozen?"

Now Tom helped the waddy haze the small batch of cattle and calves westerly. Soon they came over a gentle knoll, and he could make out a big camp fire and a chuck wagon that had been brought out to hold food and supplies. Away to the northwest more cattle were being driven in to the herd ground, and this was some comfort to Tom Wilson. He left Hall with the cattle and let the stallion canter toward the fire. And then Tom realized there were a couple of men he hadn't seen before at the campsite along with a few hands taking a quick break.

Les Aston broke away to wave Tom in, who swung down to ground hitch his reins. About Aston was a tired grimness, and he said acidly, "Those rustlers stopped at the home buildings before hittin' the herd, Tom. They killed Fred. And guess who's with them—none other than Henry Thompson. Oh, these lawmen want to ask you some questions . . ."

"I'm Marshal Bennett, Mr. Wilson."

Frowning, Tom said, "Have I seen you before?"

"You might have up at Havre. My partner is Canadian

Mountie Doug McCray. We trailed these rustlers out of Box Elder."

"Thompson, I heard, is hooked up with them. Clemet Hall said three of them were killed . . ."

"Thompson's still alive," Les Aston said.

"Then I'm goin' after him," Tom said coldly.

"Mr. Wilson, just what connection do you have with Havre lawyer Ralph Glendenning?"

"He's ranch manager, Marshal. Or at least he's supposed to be. Why?"

"We can't prove it yet, but we suspect he's mixed up with a Canuck named Pierre LaFleur," said Bennett. "These rustlers have been delivering the cattle they steal to LaFleur, who then heads them up to a packing plant to be slaughtered."

Mountie McCray said, "It is entirely possible Glendenning set this whole thing up. We found some papers on one of the dead rustlers indicating they rode up from the Nations. One of the dead men could be Will Christian, a member of the High Fives gang. Every member of this gang is a known killer."

"Then it's time," Tom threw at the Mountie, "that we see they don't kill any more. Les, I want you to pick two good men to come with us, asides yourself. Clearing now"—his probing eyes scanned the brightening sky—"and it could be some of those rustlers could be carryin' lead in them. They'll be on tired horses."

"And tired men," Marshal Bennett cut in, "make mistakes."

"Clemet," Tom called out, "I want you to cut me out that roan I like to ride. Then you head back to the home buildings and tend to Fred; reckon you can bury him up on that knoll south of the buildings. And, Marshal Bennett, we'd best put some grub into our saddlebags. As I suspect this could take some time."

"Tom," McCray said, "you could leave this up to us . . ."

"Could, but I won't. One thing for sure, none of these outlaws will give up easy . . . and Thompson's with them . . . which is all the reason I need . . ."

Back in Box Elder on this late Sunday morning, a church bell pealed as services ended. Shortly after this the saloons began opening their doors. Now past the outskirts of town rolled the stagecoach, one of the passengers surveying a town he'd seen a few times before. The death of one of his stock detectives had brought W.D. "Billy" Smith here, even though the body had already been laid to rest in the cemetery. Smith was here to get a handle on what had happened, and he was hoping there'd be someone to take over for Dunn.

By his request the coach pulled up in front of the Carbine Hotel, and he was the only passenger to dismount. After the shotgun threw down his lonely valise, Billy Smith went into the lobby to secure lodging. He glanced at the grandfather clock wedged in a corner; it was twenty of noon. Turning his valise over to the desk clerk, he went into the dining room in hopes of beating the usual crowd that availed themselves of Sunday dinner after church services.

He found a table by a side window, and the curious eyes of Vivian McCauley, who was placing silverware on a table, focused on the badge pinned inside his open vest. As he waited to be served, idly his gaze went to the framed pictures hanging from the blue-painted wall just beyond the side window.

"Aren't you . . . ah, Mr. Smith?"

"I am, ma'am." He stood up, smiling.

Vivian held out her hand, which he shook gently, and both of them sat down. "You're here because of what happened to Nick."

"To take care of whatever expenses there are."

"Oh, I'm running this hotel. I'm Vivian McCauley. Nick was a friend of mine. He was a kind man . . . didn't deserve to die the way he did. But that job he had . . ."

"Yes, a man takes undo risks at times. You know, Vivian, I

had never met Nick Dunn. He was recommended for the stock detective job by a coalition of ranchers out here. I meant to get over, but we've been hit bad by rustlers, too . . . out Miles City way . . ."

"They took a picture of Nick . . . and some cowhands. Some photographer that passed through took the picture. All because he got rid of some rustler gang." Rising, she turned and stepped along the wall and removed a framed picture from a small peg. She came back and handed the picture to Billy Smith.

"Coffee, mister—"

"Yes," he said without looking at the waitress who'd come over. For Bill Smith's eyes had veiled over in shocked disbelief at what the picture revealed to him. Half the lawmen in the West were looking for rustler and killer Starky True. The eyes of the man in the picture seemed to bore into Billy Smith's as if saying that even in death Starky had managed to avoid the snares of the law. All the while, and this was a bitter pill for him to swallow, Starky True had hooked on as one of his stock detectives.

"Is something wrong?"

Blinking, he looked across the table at Vivian. He didn't know what to say for a moment, or even if he should reveal the truth. Now all around them people were coming in to claim tables. Among them was town marshal Parker Dillingham, doffing his shapeless hat as he spotted Smith, and naturally he had to come over to claim a chair at the table.

"Doggone, Billy Smith, it's been a spell," he gushed.

"Parker, how do," he said gruffly.

"I see you're lookin' at that picture of Nick Dunn. Yessir, he is sure some hero around here."

"I'm afraid he isn't so popular down in Wyoming. This man's real name is Starky True."

"True . . . Starky True," Dillingham busted out loudly, "the gunfighter?"

"I'm afraid so," confirmed Billy Smith.

* * *

Once again Henry Thompson found himself on the run. But he wasn't the only one nursing a bullet wound, in that Jess Williams was in awful pain because of the bullet lodged in his left hip. Three had been killed—Black Jack's brother, Will, and George Musgrove and Bob Hays. The avenging anger of Black Jack Christian burned in his eyes as he had it figured that somehow the Havre lawyer had pulled a double cross. How else could you account for all those men out by that herd.

Their first stop in their flight after the shoot-out had taken them back to the N Bar's home buildings. Much to their dismay they didn't find any fresh horses in the corrals. They stopped only long enough to search for spare ammunition for their guns. Here Thompson took charge, which was the reason they had circled way to the west and were going north now. Once they were across the Canadian border, no damned lawman, he'd told them, had any jurisdiction.

"From here we can head over to the Canadian Rockies."

"A lot of open country until we reach them mountains," Three-Fingered Jack blazed back at Thompson. "What about the rest of you? Why'n hell don't we just cut to the southwest and hit the Outlaw Trail, follow it back into Nevada, maybe—"

"I'll tell you why, the lot of you," said Black Jack. "We're not cuttin' an' runnin' until things are settled. With both Glendenning and LaFleur."

"You're sayin' we was set up?"

"Somebody has got to answer for Will."

They rode on through the day, chomping on the little food they had left and resting at times. Toward late afternoon Henry Thompson allowed they were approaching the Marias River. "Bunch of little cowtowns strung along the main road between Havre and Shelby. Should find a doctor in one of them. Yeah, up at Galata."

"I'm for that," groaned out Jess Williams. He reined up and

swivelled his eyes to Black Jack, who was scanning their back trail. "See anything?"

"Just a crow taking wing."

"After that," pondered Thompson, "we could head over to where LaFleur's bunch is waitin' for us."

"Yeah, what we'll do," affirmed Black Jack. "Get to the bottom of this. Come on, let's ride." He spurred into a fast canter without so much as looking at the wounded Jess Williams in passing, lost as he was in his own personal hatred.

Nearly ten miles to the south came the two lawmen and Tom Wilson and his hands. They couldn't miss the trail left by the fleeing rustlers, and back by a water hole, smiles had appeared when they'd spotted fresh blood staining a flat rock. "I expect they feel once they cross the border they'll be safe."

Mountie Doug McCray smiled at this. "There's no border for these mad dog killers."

On the move again, and with Tom having one of his cowpokes to either side on a level stretch of prairie, his thoughts were on the rangeland they were passing over. Though their horses were still holding out, he knew in order to catch the rustlers, and even though it meant a delay, they would have to change mounts. "Osborne, northwest of here lies the W Slash F. What I want you to do is take off and tell Wilber Farley we need fresh horses. Then you bring them back up along the Marias River. If you handle this right, Sid, you should be there about the same time."

"What if these rustlers cut back to the east, Tom?"

"No towns in that direction. Thompson knows this. Nope, they'll keep striking due north."

"Hey," Marshal Bennett yelled out, "some dust comin' our way from the west—seems to be pourin' out of that draw yonder. Like a bunch of riders would make." The draw in question lay below where they were riding and was one of a series of draws gouging in an east-west direction. Uneasily they lowered their hands to their holstered guns, not at all sure of what to expect.

Suddenly a rider burst out of the draw, and instantly Marshal

Harlow Bennett exclaimed, "Hell, that's Milt Hayward, or I'm blind as a bat."

No sooner had the horseman vacated the draw, than he was in too close to get out from under the barrels of the many sixguns aimed at him. And he had no choice but to saw back and rein up his sweat-stained mount. Then his pursuers appeared and fanned out while slowing their horses. Frantically he blurted out to the marshal, "You gotta help me, Marshal Bennett, put me under your protection."

"Why should I, you damned rustler!"

Milt Hayward, hatless and sweat staining his face, shifted his eyes to Tom Wilson. "It was Glendenning hiring me to take out that stock detective, Wilson. So's he could give the job to his man, Dunn."

"Keep on babbling, Hayward, spell it out."

"I was paid by Glendenning to kill stock detective Poul Gregson. An' I reckon he's behind all this rustling, too."

"That cuts it," Tom said viciously. He looked at a rancher he knew, Kelly Riggins, and the man's hired hands looking on and still gripping their sidearms. Now Riggins spurred up and nodded curtly to Marshal Bennett. "We killed the rest of his bunch. So what's it to be, Marshal, there's a lot of cottonwoods out thisaway."

"You heard what Hayward said," Bennett muttered, as he rode in close to put manacles around the rustler's wrists. "About that Havre lawyer being involved in this. Or could he be lying?"

"No," Milt Hayward responded shakily. "I ain't. You get me into a courtroom, I'll testify against that bastard Glendenning."

"Okay," grumbled Kelly Riggins. "Just where are you boys headed anyway . . ."

Tom said, "They hit my place last night. Henry Thompson's part of this bunch. Right now they're closin' on the Marias . . . packin' one or two wounded with them."

"Kelly," Marshal Bennett said, "I'm now deputizing you and your men. First of all, I want Hayward here delivered, alive I might add, to the sheriff over at Shelby. As right now he's our only witness against this damned lawyer. I want you, Kelly, to personally take Hayward over there. An' you others, you're now deputy U.S. marshals. Okay, push 'em out."

Having been in Galata before, Henry Thompson led the others to a clapboard house a block away from the business places. The sun was low to the west, and it was around seven o'clock, and they were bone tired. As they were swinging down, a woman poked her head out the back door. Then she came out when she saw them helping Jess Williams down from his saddle.

Turning, she yelled back through the open door, "Dear, there's a wounded man out here."

"Baker, you stay here and keep an eye on things. I don't want this sawbones sneakin' off to warn any lawman." Black Jack peered westerly, knew the sun wouldn't set until after nine, but what did it matter now; they were at least for the moment at a safe haven. "Baker, tell that doctor Jess's sixgun went off accidental-like. He ain't got no reason to question that."

Gazing at the dirty bandage wrapped around Henry Thompson's forearm, Three-Fingered Jack muttered, "You could have that wound cleaned, Henry."

"To hell with it. What I want is just to plop down in a chair and slop down some cold beer. Well, Black Jack, we got this far. They could be after us, but out a long ways. Be dark a'fore long . . . and let tomorrow take care of itself."

"Yup," he said. "Be dark soon. First we'll stable our hosses . . . and maybe try to get some fresh mounts, if there's any available." The three of them rode their horses at a walk side by side, taking in the weathered buildings of Galata. "Will, he never had a chance."

"I don't think LaFleur sold us out. This was too sweet a deal for him. I know Tom Wilson; a cautious son'bitch. I got it figured that Glendenning wanted Wilson out of the way, as I figure Glendenning was pocketing a lot of N Bar money."

"Once we hook up with LaFleur, and get his story, Henry, I'm riding for Havre. To see that silver-tongued lawyer."

A quarter moon had appeared, but it didn't help much to cast back the pall of night. Yet it did reveal the horsemen huddled in close together and going over their plans to enter Galata. Farther back, and after clearing the Marias River, darkness had cut away the trail they were following. Back there Marshal Bennett had to make a decision of whether to strike for Lothair, which lay east a few miles, or head to the cowtown they were surveying under starlight.

"Les," said Tom, "you know which house Doc Rickart lives in; he has his office there, too. The outlaws will probably leave their wounded at Rickart's, an' the rest holed up in some saloon."

"What we don't want," warned Marshal Bennett, "though I know you boys want to, is to kill everybody off. We got one witness in Milt Hayward, but Milt's word has never been worth much. So, Les, and those goin' with him, try to take someone alive. I guess that's it."

Everyone set their horses into motion as they separated into two groups. At one time or another all of them, except for the lawmen, had come into Galata to wile the night away in one saloon or the other as there were only two. Tom figured it would be the Crescent Bar, since it was the bigger place and had a couple of barmaids. He knew that Henry Thompson had been here and knew the layout.

They were still south of the business places strung along a couple of quiet streets. Detouring away now were Les Aston and three others, who were loping their horses toward Doc Rickart's big clapboard house. The marshal held up a restraining hand as Aston and his men dismounted quickly and with drawn weapons came in through the back door. It wasn't a matter of more than a few minutes before Les Aston reappeared and swung into the saddle and pushed toward them.

"One's in there; still out cold from all the ether Doc Rickart used. Got a bullet wound to his hip, and he ain't goin' no place for a spell."

"Leave someone there, Les, and then hook up with us."

Aston rode back and was soon returning accompanied by two riders, and now the cavalcade rode on to bring their horses onto Main Street. The street was virtually deserted at this time of night except for a man walking toward some houses to the east. The first saloon they checked was just a hole-in-the-wall called Whitey's, and upon going in for a quick check, Tom found it was empty but for a bartender playing a game of solitaire up at the bar.

Now he knew when climbing into the saddle where the rustlers were, and his anxiety deepened as he rode along beside the marshal, whose quiet orders were instantly obeyed by about half of them easing into an alley so they could come in behind the Crescent Saloon. Next thing Tom knew they were dismounting across the street from the saloon and upstreet just a shade, this to keep their horses out of the line of fire.

. With Tom were Marshal Bennett and McCray and four others, and Tom was determined that he would be among the first to enter the saloon. As he went angling across the street, he murmured, "Lucky for us those front windows are frosted over."

"Just the lower panes, though," commented Bennett as he eased the Colt .45 out of the leather holster, to have everyone follow suit. He paused to lay on them one final word of warning. "Don't be fancy and try for a head shot. Go for the chest or gut. I figure there are four of them. Quiet night as there are no hosses tied out front. How fast you figure is this Thompson?"

"If we get the drop on them, it don't matter."

"That thought could get you killed, Osborne. These boys know what's in store for them if they're captured alive. Well, soon's my knees quit clattering we can tackle this." Marshal Bennett winked and took the step that brought him within reach of the batwings, with Tom Wilson brushing his coattails.

Quickly they were in the saloon and fanning out, and even

so, the guns of the rustlers were beginning to speak and to spit out sudden death. Only the guns of Tom Wilson and the venging men with him were deadlier, a bullet killing Sixtoes Baker where he'd risen somewhat drunkenly from a rickety wooden chair. Dunlop, the one known as Three-Fingered Jack, went down so quickly he probably didn't even know he was dead.

As more of their comrades were coming in through the back door, Tom found himself gritting his teeth when a bullet from Henry Thompson's booming gun nicked his arm. But this failed to deter Tom's deadly aim, as he just let the Colt buck in his hand, the bullets from it slamming into Thompson's mid-section and chest in a killing tattoo. Then the outlaw went crashing back to spill against the roulette wheel. When the gunsmoke cleared away from Tom's eyes, he realized all of the rustlers were dead, but his ears were still ringing from the sustained sound of gunfire.

He sagged a little, grateful that he'd survived this bloody shoot-out, gazing about, and then to his sorrow he saw that a W Slash F hand was down and lying mighty still. And the Mountie and Osborne were holding on to another cowhand.

In the spreading silence the bartender finally got the nerve to take a look from where he had dropped behind the bar. Wordlessly he began reaching to the back bar for bottles and placing them along the bar. Marshal Bennett, noticing this, moved over, and then others followed. But before he joined them, Tom sent someone to fetch the doctor. Holstering his gun, he noticed that his hand was trembling a little.

"Half of our job is done," Mountie Doug McCray announced quietly. "I still have to go after those Canucks. And there's this Havre lawyer."

"Yup," Tom enjoined bitterly, "there's Glendenning." The whiskey tasted flat going down, but he drank some more just to ease the pain of all of this.

FOURTEEN

Three weeks later, Tom Wilson witnessed the hanging of three men who'd been involved in the rustling. Where outlaws Jess Williams and Milt Hayward went to their deaths with a calm acceptance of their guilt, defrocked lawyer Ralph Glendenning had to be carried up the gallows steps, where even here a chair had to be placed under him, and so he died.

Weary of all that had happened, Tom Wilson took the stage-coach back down to Box Elder. Last week he had gotten a letter from the absentee owners of the N Bar N, asking him if he wanted to buy the ranch, and at a decent price. This was on his mind when the stage came rolling into a town he knew so well. But this thought was shoved aside through his concern for Vivian McCauley.

Her association with Nick Dunn, though it hadn't been all that serious, had gotten her branded as a shameless hussy after word had gotten around that Dunn was really the notorious outlaw Starky True. The word that had come up to Tom while testifying at the trial going on in Havre, was that Vivian had quit her job as manager of the Carbine Hotel and would be leaving Montana.

A good woman like Vivian is hard to find. Especially out in places like this. Buyin' the N Bar would have little meaning unless . . . Tom just couldn't get himself to admit that he loved Vivian McCauley. Or was it that he feared she would spurn his love.

As the driver veered closer to the boardwalk, Tom could see

through the side door window that Vivian was one of those
about to depart on it as the stage continued on down to Great
Falls. When it pulled up, he was the first to dismount. He could
come back to get his luggage later, for now there was little time
to waste. He found Vivian returning his smile, and then he simply took a firm grip on her arm and walked her, to her bewil-
derment, back up the sidewalk in the direction of the bank.

"I'm not playin' the fool any longer, Vivian." He paused to
sweep the Stetson from his head. Turning to face her squarely,
he added with a questioning smile tugging at his mouth, "I
love you, I reckon I always have."

"Tom, you know what they've been saying," she blurted
out.

"Do you think I want just any woman to marry me, I—"

"What did you say?"

"First of all, that I'm goin' over to the bank to try and buy
the N Bar. And, yes, will you marry me—"

"Oh, Tom, gladly, and with all my heart."

Now that the long narration of W.D. "Billy" Smith had finally ended, he gazed around at those clustered about him in
the barroom of the Owen Wister Hotel in Buffalo, Wyoming
Territory. They had hung on his every word, but still he knew
as fellow lawmen they always wanted that final piece of proof
that would end the saga of Starky True.

Reaching under his coat, he brought out the picture he had
removed from the wooden frame up in the Carbine Hotel in
Box Elder. And he simply placed it on the table as he rose, to
head for the bar and let his fellow lawmen study the evidence.

He had another shot glass of brandy, cocking his ears to
their expressions of belief now in all that he had said, and then
Billy Smith simply walked out of the barroom and went outside to reclaim his horse. His job here was done, and he knew
the picture of Starky True would be reframed and hung along

with others in the historic hotel he was leaving behind. If he pushed it a little, he could make Sheridan by nightfall.

Then on to Montana and back to the arduous task of hunting down more lawbreakers. He couldn't help saying as he cleared the outskirts of Buffalo, "Starky, you might have made a fine lawman. But now you're legend . . ."

THE BLOOD BOND SERIES

by William W. Johnstone

The continuing adventures of blood brothers, Matt Bodine and Sam Two Wolves — two of the fastest guns in the west.

BLOOD BOND	(2724, $3.95)
BLOOD BOND #2: BROTHERHOOD OF THE GUN	(3044, $3.95)
BLOOD BOND #3: GUNSIGHT CROSSING	(3473, $3.95)
BLOOD BOND #4: GUNSMOKE AND GOLD	(3664, $3.50)
BLOOD BOND #5: DEVIL CREEK CROSSFIRE	(3799, $3.50)
BLOOD BOND #6: SHOOTOUT AT GOLD CREEK	(4222, $3.50)
BLOOD BOND #7: SAN ANGELO SHOOTOUT	(4466, $3.99)

Available wherever paperbacks are sold, or order direct from the Publisher. Send cover price plus 50¢ per copy for mailing and handling to Penguin USA, P.O. Box 999, c/o Dept. 17109, Bergenfield, NJ 07621. Residents of New York and Tennessee must include sales tax. DO NOT SEND CASH.